THE OUTING

Jack Douglas

Copyright © 2021 Jack Douglas

All rights reserved

The characters and events portrayed in this book are fictitious. Any similarity to real persons, living or dead, is coincidental and not intended by the author.

No part of this book may be reproduced, or stored in a retrieval system, or transmitted in any form or by any means, electronic, mechanical, photocopying, recording, or otherwise, without express written permission of the publisher.

ISBN-13: 9798466990355
ISBN-10: 1477123456

Cover design by: Art Painter
Library of Congress Control Number: 2018675309
Printed in the United States of America

Dedication
This book is dedicated, to older people who have suffered, more than most, from the coronavirus and the lockdowns. I'm hoping that it will bring a bit of laughter to a troubled world.

Acknowledgements
I would like to express my appreciation to the following people who assisted me in writing of this book;
My wife Susan for putting up with me again whilst I worked on this book.
My sons David and Alan for their encouragement as always.
Again, I would like to thank my lifelong friend Gary Armstrong for all his valuable help and suggestions
Thank you to you all.
JD

PREFACE

The Outing

The residents (inmates) of the Candlewick Manor care home have an unusual way of conducting themselves. It seems that the free market economy is alive and well and thriving at the Manor as it is known. The fact that a few corners have to be cut and that the government, local authority and social services all have to pay for the mess the care sector is currently in, is fair game to the staff and inmates at the Manor. In spite of official visits to see what they do with all of the grants and donations the staff at the Manor are able to see off various investigations.

The Outing is about a care home with a difference. Although the inmates are all 'getting on' a bit they have not lost their zest for life but rather embrace it in a life affirming way and by never giving a sucker and even break.

From the embarrassingly large cash surpluses to the extra-curricular, 'little earners' everyone at the Manor is relatively well off to the point where excess cash needs to be spent on something. As an Outing is planned each year then it seems only sensible to use some of the surplus funds in paying for the Outing.

This year's Outing is to Whitby and no expense has been spared. However this does not stop break-away groups deciding to organise trips within trips. One lot end up at the Redcar races and another lot seeks adventure in Robin Hood's bay. A potential visit to Dracula's grave doesn't get off the ground but even the Remainers group, that stay in Whitby, manage to wreak havoc on the unsuspecting locals and find it difficult to stay out of trouble.

Each of the groups have far too good a time and the sparks start to fly, in more ways than one, when they all converge back again at Whitby for a well-earned fish and chip supper.

The coach journeys to and from Whitby are endured with some intrepidation and the inmates take the opportunity for a bit of nostalgia when discussing the various topics of the day. Sometimes the lively exchange of views may get a bit heated but it all works out in the end and some interesting philosophical observations are made.

The inmates are very vocal in their somewhat traditional opinions and are very un-PC in some of their remarks. Their comments are sometimes a reflection on the world we live in today and they manage to make their points in a funny and witty way.

Following the Outing the police investigate the goings on that have been reported to them finding it hard to believe that a bunch of geriatrics could behave like juvenile delinquents. The police return to follow up the hooliganism and other matters that have come to their attention.

Although the inmates 'sail close to the wind' in some of their activities, and can behave in such mischievous ways, they all have a gentle humour and believe in living life to the full.

This book is entirely a work of fiction. The names, characters and incidents in it are the work of the author's imagination. Any resemblance to actual persons, living or dead, events or organisations is entirely coincidental.

Nor do any of the organisations bear any resemblance to real organisations and are generally fictitious. Other than the fact that such situations and organisations can exist in any large city. Similarly the places in Whitby do actually exist but everything else is entirely made up.

This is the third novel by Jack Douglas who is married and has two grown up sons and lives in the Midlands. The coronavirus lockdowns have provided the time to complete this work of fiction. It is completely made up and has been written for a bit of fun to hopefully raise a smile for anyone who has suffered under the lockdowns.

CHAPTER 1

Monday, the week of the Outing

"Now do come along Mr Johnson," said Nurse Chastity Brown as she tried to get a reluctant Mr Johnson into the shower.

"I've told you I don't need a wash!" exclaimed Mr Johnson.

"We have a shower every day don't we? Whether we need it or not." replied the nurse somewhat exasperated.

Eventually, after much cajoling, encouragement and the odd bit of praise, Mr Johnson did indeed take a shower assisted by the nurse. He complained continually throughout the process and said that he thought it most unreasonable that he was required to undergo such practices every day.

The nurse commiserated with him and said, "there we are, all done now. That wasn't so bad was it?"

"Thank goodness for that," said Mr Johnson, not the easiest of the current inhabitants of the old peoples home where he resided but one of those that still retained most of his faculties.

So started a new week at the 'Home for Retired Gentlefolk' as the advertising information described it.

This old people's home had been established several years ago by a philanthropist widow who left her total inheritance to the Home, much to the anger and frustration of her children. It was a large, old Victorian house which would have originally housed a family of some importance as it had a number of fairly big rooms and originally there was stabling for coaches and horses in the adjoining yard. Locally known as the Manor because it was a house of some importance that could have potentially befitted a Lord of the Manor. In fact a family of industrialists had christened it a Manor house when they had first occupied it.

It was clear that the servants attending the original owners would have occupied the downstairs areas and looked after deliveries and the kitchen and storage areas. The main living rooms originally occupying the middle floor whilst the 'family's' sleeping quarters were on the upper floors.

Several owners since then had brought the house up to date with regard to plumbing and electrics and such like. A garage block had been added and the front garden had been converted into a car park for about a dozen or so cars.

So when the house had come onto the market few years ago now it was snapped up by the philanthropist widow and converted to an old people's home for gentlefolk. However the widow passed away not long after owing thousands and thousands of pounds for work that had been carried out on the home, most of which had not really been fully completed due to unscrupulous builders.

The house was put up for sale in order to settle the widow's debts and a company called the Care Home Company or CHC for short bought it lock, stock and barrel as they say.

CHC did have a couple of other homes in other parts of the country, but this was the first one north of the Midlands. Each home was run on an autonomous basis with the manager having complete control. The company was supposed to be a charity, but with the situation in the UK, regarding how the costs for the elderly should be paid for, being in such a mess, the company was able to exploit this and turn a tidy profit as well. A lot of this was due to the manager of this particular home, Ajay Chowdhury, and his accountant, Henry.

By carefully dividing and partitioning the rooms and upgrading the kitchen and central heating CHC managed to accommodate about thirty residents/inmates (inmates was the expression given to the old people living in the Home by the staff as a sort of joke – likening it to a prison). As the inhabitants didn't really mind what they were called the term just seemed to stick when the staff, and on occasion others, were talking about them. Although it wasn't supposed to be like a prison it was run with a certain amount of discipline instilled by the matron of the home. 'The Matron', as she liked to be known, was what would be termed 'old school' having worked her way up through the NHS until retirement. Now in her sixties she was a formidable woman and woe betide anyone who didn't do as they were told straightaway!

Of the thirty or so inhabitants of the Home there were a number of what are colloquially known as 'characters'. These are people who everyone knows and likes in spite of their idiosyncrasies. They are eccentric to the point of, well sort of, backing into another type of normality, sometimes devoid of any relation to the actual current reality.

As Mr Johnson went down to his breakfast on that Monday morning, he wondered why Nurse Chastity Brown was so formal when everyone else called him Bert. Most people thought this was short for Albert but Mr Johnson's first name was actually Cuthbert but he tended to keep that quiet as he didn't want anyone thinking he was posh and therefore loaded with money. He was, actually, too fond of the betting on the horse races to be 'well off' anyway.

Nurse Chastity Brown had arrived in England, with her family, from the Caribbean some years ago now as a child. She trained as a nurse with the NHS and was recruited by the Matron a year or so ago. As a nurse she worked closely with the Matron and helped dispense medication as well as helping some of the more 'difficult' inmates wash, take showers and get dressed. Bert was one such inmate that she helped not because of any physical aspect but because Bert could be so stubborn sometimes that he wouldn't wash or get dressed just because he didn't want to.

Bert was known as one of the 'characters' of the Home and Harry the handyman always placed his bets for him and although Bert was as cantankerous as they come, he and Harry always got on well and could talk for hours about different racecourses and various trainers and jockeys. Both Bert and Harry believed that betting on horses was a skill and nothing to do with chance whatsoever. If you managed to match the right trainer and jockey with a 'good' horse then you simply couldn't fail. The trouble was no one had told the bookies this and Bert and Harry couldn't understand while most of the time their selections were still running long after the race had finished.

On his way to have breakfast Bert bumped into The General, a military bearing chap who had been in the forces for years before having retirement forced upon him. The General, as he was always referred to, had never really got over leaving the army and still thought those people around him were inferior ranks and could therefore be bossed about. He came unstuck on more than one occasion following such an assumption. No one really knew if he had, in fact, been a general, it was what he had always been called ever since arriving at the Home and everyone was just used to calling him that now.

"How goes it Bert?" enquired the General.

"No so bad General how are you, and, more importantly, is there anything in the three thirty at Kempton, this afternoon, that you fancy?" replied Bert.

"Not had time to study the form yet, old boy, but Harry should be about soon with the daily paper," and with that, Bert and the General moved off into the dining room.

CHAPTER 2

Breakfast is served

The dining room was on the ground floor of the big old house with the kitchen and food preparations areas adjoining it. The kitchen had been extended considerably into the yard and back garden areas to allow for deliveries round the back of the Home.

Originally the Home had been called the Complete Retirement for Aged Peoples Home. However when abbreviated this became the C.R.A.P Home and so that name was changed rather hastily to The Old Peoples Establishment Manor, unfortunately the abbreviation of this (T.O.P. EM) sounded more like an advert for euthanasia than an old peoples home.

So it was finally decided to refer to the Home by the original name given to the house when it was first built well over a hundred years ago – Candlewick Manor. The original owners being in the candle making trade. Consequently it tended to be referred to just as the 'Manor' these days.

"Is your Grandson coming in to see you today?" enquired Old Joe as he buttered another piece of toast.

"Not today dear," replied Gertie just finishing he eggs royale.

Both Old Joe (who was probably the youngest inhabitant there) and Gertie (short for Gertrude), who was probably one of the oldest, were not particularly long-term inmates, having been at the Home for about three years now. Old Joe was called 'old' to differentiate himself from Young Joe, who, in a perverse way, was a good twenty years older than Old Joe. Neither Joe minded very much and people soon got used to this odd way of addressing them.

Gertrude or Gertie as she preferred to be called was a very posh older lady. Some said she was related to the Queen and Gertie liked to encourage this misconception. She had once been married to some minor aristocrat who had run off with one of the chambermaids many years ago leaving Gertie a 'bit short' on the financial front. Still Bert and Harry tended to pass the odd racing tip to her which helped in making ends meet.

Gertie's grandson also helped supplement her income by supplying paper products to the Home. Mainly toilet rolls, tissues and big sheets of paper used for medical examination tables, but which were used as tablecloths at the Manor. No one knew where he got the stuff from or how he could afford to sell it so cheaply but, as the Home, and Gertie's grandson were both happy with the arrangement then it was generally considered best just to let it carry on. Although it hadn't always been that way. When Gertie had first moved into the Manor Home, she didn't like it because they were all 'old' and she asked Terry to get her out of the Manor and take her somewhere where they weren't so old. Terry said, "you need to give it a go Nan, you know a few weeks. If you still don't like it after that then we'll find somewhere else."

Like most older people who find change such a strain Gertie found it difficult to adjust at first, as she had been independent for a number of years. She did however settle down very well, and after a relatively short time, and she was almost considered to be like one of the founders of the Home now.

Gertie was saying, "such a nice boy, my grandson – Terry, and always takes an interest in what everyone is doing."

"That's because he can get you anything you want for a price – no questions asked," muttered Old Joe.

"What's that dear? I didn't quite hear you," said Gertie.

"I was just saying that that's nice and asking after him," replied Old Joe.

"Oh, he's fine. I dare say he'll be in again later in the week. I think he's got some make-up and underwear for Beryl," said Gertie completely straight faced.

The inmates were sitting at round tables that each seated four people. Most of the tables were occupied and the inmates were tucking into cereals, toast and marmalade which was the usual weekday breakfast. At weekends cooked breakfasts were provided, eggs, sausages and bacon if they were allowed it. Many of the inmates had to make do with boiled or poached eggs because of medical conditions although a few did manage the 'Full English' as it was referred to. Gertie didn't let petty rules and regulations, like what to have for breakfast, bother her and insisted on eggs royale or eggs benedict every day regardless.

"What's that! What's that you're saying?" shouted Beryl from the next table. Like most of the inmates her hearing suffered as she had got older. Although many of the inmates should really be wearing hearing aids, they seldom bothered being too vain to wear the things. Consequently there was usually a great deal of shouting to accompany any meal they had.

"I was just saying dear, that my grandson, Terry will be bringing in your underwear later in the week," replied Gertie loud enough for the whole room to hear.

All talking stopped and everyone looked towards Gerties and Beryl's tables waiting for Beryl's response. Gertie's grandson Terry was in his twenties and Beryl was rapidly approaching eighty and so the idea of Terry having Beryl's underwear greatly intrigued the inmates who eagerly waited to hear how this had come about.

"Oh, good, I hope he's not late again like he was last time when he delivered my surgical stockings. I've just about wore out the stuff I've got on and it keeps rising up you know? I've been meaning to get some new under garments for some time now," Beryl said as she fidgeted in a meaningful way so as to emphasise the point about her underwear rising up.

There was a loud exhale as everyone went back to eating their breakfasts the scent of scandal disappearing like an early morning mist.

Beryl was in good condition for her age and she didn't mind people knowing it. She was very outspoken and blunt to the point of being just plain rude. She didn't mince her words or suffer fools gladly and her biggest gripe was people mumbling when they spoke to her. She was frequently heard to remark why can't people speak up when I'm talking to them. She was quite a big, boisterous lady who definitely liked her food and drink.

Just then the General and Bert arrived and said their "Good Mornings" to as many inmates as caught their eyes. The General moved off to sit with Young Joe and Cyril both being similar in age and both having been in the forces themselves. Although Young Joe didn't say a great deal, Cyril more than made up for this as he was a constant talker. He had a fund of funny stories and liked a joke but the problem was he just wouldn't shut up, at all, and sometimes this verbal diarrhoea got him into trouble with the other inmates. Cyril's main career had been with the police and he had risen through the ranks over the years. The trouble was now he was apt to forget he was no longer still in the police and so his threats to arrest anyone who upset him needed to be met with good humour and a pat on the back.

Young Joe was one of the oldest inhabitants and was a big bear like man who looked to have been strong in his youth. Although he had played a lot of sports when he was younger his occupation was that of an accountant and his son Henry, the Home's accountant, is now following in his footsteps. Young Joe doesn't usually say very much but he can be a bit of a 'dark horse'.

Peggy, another fairly long term inmate, went to join Gertie and Old Joe and let out an enormous fart as she sat down. "Hark at me," she said, completely unfazed. "Must have been the beans on toast last night making themselves known," she added with a laugh.

Both Gertie and Old Joe had pulled a bit of a face but Peggy just smiled and said, "are you both looking forward to Friday?"

Gertie and Old Joe looked at each other and said together, "Friday? What's happening on Friday?"

Peggy looked surprised and said, "don't tell me you've forgotten the annual Outing."

Gertie and old Joe looked at each with blank expressions on their faces as they tried to recall what had been said about this year's outing. Like most of the inmates their memory wasn't what it should have been and the beginnings of memory failure of one sort or another was present in most older people. They insisted that they just needed a bit of a nudge to get the brain cells firing on all cylinders again. Generally the inmates at the Manor were a lot more active and kept their faculties longer than others of their age mainly because of the funding the Manor was able to enjoy. There were, of course, the odd senile moments as they were called but everyone was usually in pretty good spirits and they all tended to get on well enough with each other.

Peggy continued, "It's the annual Outing – you know the day trip to the seaside!"

Beryl shouted across, "that's not this Friday its next week."

"No," said Peggy, "I've just been looking at the notice board and it's definitely this Friday."

One or two of the residents rushed out to check the notice board and there, sure enough, was the notice saying that this coming Friday there would be a day trip to Whitby.

"Well I just hope it's better than last year's trip to Skegness. I'm not kidding you but if the world had piles that's where they'd be!" exclaimed Old Joe.

"Oh I suffer from them," said Bert to a chorus of 'me too's' from the others that had congregated around the notice board.

CHAPTER 3

Later that day - Another scam for Henry

Henry was the accountant for the Manor and he was also the son of one of the inmates. Young Joe had been an accountant and Henry followed in his footsteps. As his dad suffered slightly from dementia Henry tended to just pop in and see him and then proceed to the main purpose of his visit, 'doing a bit of business' with the manager, Ajay, as he would say to his dad, Young Joe.

It was just after lunch when he was able to discuss the latest profit forecasts with Ajay. Ajay always invited Henry to join him for lunch in the dining room at the Home but Henry always declined. It wasn't so much the food that he didn't like (in fact the food was very good to the point of being quite remarkable for an old peoples home) but it was the way the inmates ate it. All of them were getting on in years now and very few had all of their own teeth and it just put him off his food when people removed their dentures at the table because a bit of food was stuck. The noises as well were not exactly conducive to enjoying the meal as there seemed to be an awful lot of effort to consume even basic fare such as soup.

Henry was not only a qualified accountant but thought of himself as an entrepreneur, which was a polite way of saying that he did a bit of 'ducking and diving', what he, and others, referred to as 'little earners'. It didn't get dodgier than this unless a person was an estate agent on the side.

Henry and Ajay had made quite a lot of money out of the

Manor not all of the profits being repatriated to the parent company, CHC. Together with Ajay's assistant manager Brenda and Betty the bookkeeper the four of them were on a private enterprise crusade to liberate funds from whatever source they could exploit. The subsequent surpluses were always welcome and deployed in various ways and everyone, well everyone in the Home, benefitted.

The Manor fully exploited the current mess the social healthcare sector was in. The NHS considered it a local authority responsibility and the local authority considered it to be the NHS responsibility. The government were basically sitting on the side-lines hoping the problem would go away and had foolishly placed the problem with social services. The resultant mess meant that care homes for the elderly were either outrageously expensive or notoriously under-funded due to various inefficiencies propagated by the different agencies involved.

The Manor took advantage of such a mess and proceeded to fleece whichever organisation they could, although it was ostensibly financed as a charity, plus whatever grants that it received. With Henry's typical determination he found more exciting ways to fiddle as much money as he could out of the government, the local authority and social services. He considered the NHS had enough problems and so, with a Robin Hood halo, tended to leave them alone.

Henry would frequently remark that 'they were asking for it'. "If they can't get this lot organised to provide adequate social care for the elderly, after all of the years they've been messing about with it, then they obviously can't be trusted in looking after whatever money they do have and so we'll look after it for them!"

Both Henry and Ajay thought it was their moral duty that the inmates at the Manor shouldn't suffer at the hands of such inadequate bureaucrats who bleated on and on about insufficient resources whilst wasting tons of money on pointless politically correct agendas without actually getting anything done. The number of times one faceless bureaucrat after another appeared on television talking a load of rubbish just became a joke to them and so they thought that if ever there was a situation worth exploiting then this was it!

There was only one problem with these arrangements that Henry made and that was it produced a lot of cash, even after Ajay and Henry had taken their 'legitimate performance bonuses' there was lots of surplus cash. This was where Brenda and Betty came into their own. Brenda for innovative ways of using the money and Betty for her esoteric bookkeeping which made 'following the money' a bit of a non-starter for anyone trying to audit the books.

Brenda was saying, "the Outing on Friday will be a good way of using some of this month's surplus. We've hired the best coach we can again. It's not just a charabanc, you know? We've also got the tour guide Wayne and the driver Derick who we've used before."

Ajay said, "well, I know we've used this coach firm before and whilst the coaches themselves are usually good the driver and tour guides have not always been, shall we say, quite what we expected?"

"Oh, I think they'll be alright. Both Derick and Wayne are slightly on the odd side – what one might refer to as departures from the evolutionary mainstream – but their hearts are in the right place and they'll look after the inmates and get them there and back safely and that's the main thing," said Brenda.

"OK," said Ajay, "we'll see how it goes. Provided they get them there and back safely then that's OK."

"Will you be going this year?" asked Henry.

Ajay started to say that he went every year, but Brenda and Betty looked at him knowing full well that he always put his name down to go but always found an excuse to back out of the outing at the last minute.

Ajay eventually said, "I'm hoping to go Henry, but you know how it is, the demands on my time and such like I can't always get away."

Brenda and Betty just nodded all were thinking that Ajay will find an excuse to back out once again.

Ajay went on, "we've arranged lunch and dinner and various activities in Whitby itself. You know the sort of thing, we'll sort out visits to museums and exhibitions. They'll like that the inmates will, although five minutes later most of them won't remember a thing. But although that will get rid of this month's surplus, we can't keep doing this on a piece-meal basis. I mean we've hired in the latest films and entertainers, in the past, plus some private medical staff for different treatments and all that costs a lot. It doesn't seem to matter what we do, we always end up with a massive surplus at the end of the month. Although no one seems bothered about it and we keep passing any audits that come our way. So we have a hefty surplus in the bank and we'll need to sort out some longer term solutions where to put it soon otherwise someone's going to start asking questions soon about where all the money is coming from!"

Betty said, "it's all recorded in my bookkeeping system."

Henry just looked at Betty and said, "well it's the government's own fault if they can't get their act together. There are so many different rules and regulations and benefits and grants to be had and they are so complicated that no one really understands then. You need to be a rocket scientist just to complete some of the forms! So the trick is to apply for everything you can and several times over then the law of averages says you're going to be onto a number of 'winners'."

Ajay added reflectively, "well at least our inmates don't have to sell their houses to live here at the Manor. Which is just as well I suppose because nearly all of them are able to chip in from renting out their properties and most of them are up to some sort of scam or other as well. We're lucky that we have such an understanding clientele and that they support such free market activities."

"I know for a fact that most of your inmates as you tend to call them like a bet on the horses and they also dabble in a bit of buying and selling. In fact most of the supplies come through this way. I have trouble getting receipts for everything," replied Henry looking at Ajay. "Mind you Betty does a good job in disguising any dodgy dealings. You know she has the most remarkable book-keeping system that I have ever seen!"

"This still isn't solving our problem of what to do with all the surpluses we generate!" said Ajay.

"No, well I've been thinking about that and I think I may have come up with a solution," said Henry.

"Go on," said Ajay, "let's hear your latest scam.

"Please," said Henry, "it's an investment proposal."

Ajay just nodded as Henry went onto explain his latest brainwave of creating specialist limited companies known as Special Purpose Vehicles (SPVs). These would then be used to 'park' the surplus cash. Bonds would then be sold in respect of the 'streams of income' available to the SPVs and this money, in effect, can be reinvested or just banked offshore somewhere until Ajay and Henry decided what to do with it.

"Hmm," said Ajay, "it sounds like a plan. I mean we can't just up and have it away with a ton of surplus money, as much as we might like to, but this can muddy the waters sufficiently so that no one will be able to see just how well off we are."

"Also," continued Henry, "the inmates and staff can buy into the bonds as well and so this will tie them in to the scheme and it should fit in well with all the other little earners, as they call them, which are going on."

Brenda and Betty just nodded, and Ajay concluded, "this will make being able to differentiate what's the Manor's money and what's ours and what's theirs extremely difficult so everyone should come out it that much richer – let's do it!"

CHAPTER 4

The Inmates Activities

Monday passed very quickly as word spread about the impending Outing this coming Friday. Everyone was blaming everyone else for getting the dates wrong. The staff at the Manor believed that it had always been this specific Friday but the inmates firmly believed that date had been changed. So there was a certain amount of agitation as most of the inmates started their preparation almost immediately for their trip in a few days' time.

This mix up with dates also played havoc with the extra-curricular scams that the inmates tended to indulge in, and threw out potential deliveries and the like.

One particular inmate, Elizabeth, who played the stock market like a fiddle, which it was really to her, as her granddaughter Rebecca, worked for a firm of stockbrokers. Between Elizabeth and Rebecca they had shared a few 'windfalls' to use their expression.

Elizabeth was quite a posh, elderly lady, who had recently fallen on hard times. She always took time over her appearance and was frequently heard to say that she thought that standards were falling all over and that it had to stop. She had a big house down South somewhere that she rented out and with the income from that and this little investment side-line she was managing very nicely now.

Every Friday her daughter would bring in the Financial Times so that it didn't look odd that she was making money out of her investments in shares. After all it looked like Elizabeth was studying the market and so was bound to come up with some substantial gains from time to time. Her granddaughter, Rebecca, was an adviser on share tips, and her column on investments appeared in several of the Sunday newspapers. The idea they concocted was for Elizabeth to buy on the Friday and then sell again on the Monday after the share price has increased due to the press coverage that her granddaughter has arranged. This was all carried out through nominated accounts so as to make it difficult to follow their transactions should anyone start making enquiries about what they are up to.

So Elizabeth says to her friend, Mary, "I'm a little bit bothered that the Outing is taking place this Friday. It doesn't really give Rebecca and me time to sort out alternative arrangements."

Mary, who's not too sure exactly what Elizabeth and her granddaughter get up to just says, "never mind, I'm sure you can catch up with things the following week."

Elizabeth just gave her a withering look as she goes to call Rebecca.

Bert, Gertie and the General were also a bit put out because the betting system that they were playing involves Harry going to the bookmakers each day and as they will all be at the Outing on Friday then they will not be able to play their 'system'.

"I don't know what we'll do on Friday," Bert was saying to Gertie and the General as Harry walked up to them.

Gertie said, "I need a couple of decent wins to help Terry out in buying some surplus stock. He's got an opportunity to get his hands on some top of the range designer clothes."

"I thought he tended to nick the stuff?" said the General as Gertie gave him a look that could kill at fifty paces.

Harry said, "why don't we have the day at the races? Redcar's only about twenty odd miles up the road from Whitby and we could be there for the afternoon's racing and back for the fish and chip supper, they're organising, before they even know we've gone!"

All three of them stopped and looked at Harry as though he had just landed from outer space.

"D'ye think we can do it without anyone finding out?" asked the General clearly excited as he tended to revert to a Scottish lilt whenever something slightly out of the ordinary was mentioned.

"I'm sure we can, it'll just take a bit of organising that's all. I'll find out who would be up for it and look into how we can get from Whitby to Redcar," said Harry.

"Discreetly, mind Harry, discreetly" said Bert, "we don't want all and sundry coming along now do we?"

"Oh, I'll be discrete alright, just you leave it to me," and with that Harry wondered off to set about organising a day trip within a day trip.

Gertie said that she would be getting in touch with her grandson, Terry, to see if he would like to come to the races on Friday with them. As they were allowed to take family members and friends with them on the Outing, she thought Terry might like a day out from all the hustle and bustle of the buying and selling that he got up to.

Meanwhile, in a separate part of the Home, Eric, the care manager, and Cyril were having a discussion in respect of supplies for the outing.

Cyril was saying, "it's not so much having a drink on the way there although some of them will like to get into the swing of things early, no it's more for on the way back. You know they'll like to have a sing-song and they'll welcome a drink after a hard day at the seaside."

Eric said, "I dunno, Cyril, you know what some of this lot are like once they've got a drink inside of them."

"I'll take full responsibility," said Cyril still thinking he was 'on the job'.

"I tell you what, let me have a word with Betty and see how much 'float' I can get for the carers. Once we know how much we've got to play with we can work out what to get. How does that sound?"

Cyril's eyes were shining in anticipation of a good booze up and said, "great Eric, thanks. I'll liaise with you later in the week," and with that walked off to phone his granddaughter Rebecca. As Elizabeth's granddaughter was also called Rebecca, Cyril's granddaughter was referred to as Becky so as to avoid confusion. It didn't really help as a state of confusion was the normal situation for most of the inmates most of the time.

Becky had joined the police force at about the same time as Cyril was retiring. She was still in uniform, and Cyril was certain she would welcome a day out. Cyril thought back to when he first joined as a copper on the beat all those years ago. Not like today he thought, no respect now, you don't know what you are likely to come up against, knives, guns, all sorts, and he worried about the future in general and Becky in particular. It just wasn't the same job as when he'd joined. These days if the police make an arrest using a bit of force then it's automatically assumed they are in the wrong and the perpetrator is in the right. No, it's all wrong thought Cyril as he called Becky.

Another group were also busy making plans for their outing. This was mainly due to Elizabeth who, in addition to worrying about her share tips, had got it into her head that they would be able to go and see Robin Hood at Robin Hood's Bay. In spite of the best efforts by some of the inmates to try and convince her that Robin Hood was no longer around, Elizabeth was adamant that she was going to see him.

With a commitment to optimism that was commendable beyond belief, Elizabeth had convinced Beryl and Mary to come with her. A great deal of subterfuge would be called for, once they got to Whitby, so that they could slip away unbeknown to the others. Elizabeth's granddaughter Rebecca would come and a break would do her good thought Elizabeth. The only thing was how to work their stock market scam if they were both on the coach on Friday morning. Elizabeth thought that Rebecca will no doubt work something out and place the buy orders perhaps on the Thursday in respect of the stock to be tipped in her granddaughters Sunday newspapers columns.

Elizabeth thought that with a bit of persuading she could get the carers Mo and Priya to also come along which could prove to be a useful bit of support if anything went wrong. Perhaps Cyril would also come with them. It would be nice to have a bloke 'on the team' thought Elizabeth especially an ex-copper who can keep an eye on things.

A third group had heard that Whitby had long been associated with Dracula, the count who arrived by ship from Transylvania to feast on the blood of the unsuspecting locals. There was a rumour that Dracula was buried in the old church there. This group didn't seem to have a definitive leader and the debate rattled around quite a few of the inmates as the idea began to crystallise about visiting the grave.

Initially the debate was very positive and received a good deal of support from about half a dozen of the inmates but as talk of the visit to the grave started to take shape one or two began to get a bit worried about interfering with the supernatural. This then developed into the potential for all sorts of bad things happening to anyone who came across the grave, reminiscent to Shakespeare's grave in Stratford that threatens dire consequence on anyone who should 'disturb his bones'.

After having 'put the wind up' each other, for quite a while, it was decided not to mess with matters that they didn't understand, and which may lead to some of the inmates having nightmares, and so they concluded that it was better to leave the grave well alone.

There were various other sub-groups forming and disbanding and then reforming again as the inmates jostled for what would make the Outing extra special this year. The majority of the inmates in the end settled for the planned coach trip to Whitby, a packed lunch on the beach, perhaps a bit of a paddle in the sea and then the fish and chip supper before heading home with a drink or two to have on the coach on the way back. Most would be perfectly content with that – or so they thought- unaware of the two sub-groups which would be making additional arrangements.

CHAPTER 5

Routine days at the Manor

The carers, at the Manor, consisted of Eric and Mo (short for Maureen) and Priya and they were all experienced carers having been in the profession for quite a few years now. The staff at the Manor included the carers, Ajay, the manager, his deputy Brenda, Betty the bookkeeper, Harry the handyman, the Matron, Nurse Chastity Brown, a cook called Burnt Offering (due to his (lack of?) catering skills) and two others who filled in wherever required. One tended to act as an administrator/storeman odd job type person, called Leeroy, who had been the given the title of store manager and the other was mainly the cleaner, the 'gofer' and she also acted as assistant to Burnt Offering. She was called Sharon and, unfortunately, not the 'sharpest knife in the drawer'.

The carers were 'on the front line' so to speak and worked very hard. However the Manor was one of the better paid establishments and so the carers were more fortunate than others in their profession. Betty made sure that no one went short at the Manor. Betty had the most unusual double entry bookkeeping system which even Henry the accountant struggled to keep up with. She could turn a profit into a loss, at the drop of a hat, and disguise whatever needed to be disguised so that all the expenditure looked legitimate – at least on the surface.

Of the thirty or so inmates/residents currently at the Manor Care Home, there was a slight majority in favour of the women. Men did not tend to last as long as women these days although some of the ones in residence tended to be of a ripe old age, except for Old Joe of course who was still in his sixties – just about.

Mo and Priya tended to look after the women although Peggy always asked for Eric to help her. She called Eric, 'Jim' for some reason and however many times Eric reminded her of his real name she always called him Jim.

On the occasion the staff were given name badges, Eric showed his name badge to Peggy which clearly showed his name was Eric. Peggy looked at it for a while and then said, "that's very nice Jim."

Each of the staff had their allotted residents to attend to, which very often consisted of getting them up out of bed and getting them washed and dressed ready to have some breakfast. These simple procedures which most people take for granted can be quite a chore when people are 'getting on' in age and a great deal of patience and encouragement is usually needed. Many of the inmates tend to suffer from memory loss and in some cases it may well be the beginning of dementia. But they get by and that's the main thing. The one thing the staff at the Home can't deny is the general enthusiasm for life and the uplifting spirit that most of the inmates, at the Manor, possess. Inmates is a term of endearment rather than being derogatory and is a bit of a joke amongst the staff and residents alike.

There is a gentle humour about the place and occasions arise when staff are amused at the antics of the inmates. Like the time Mary reported that her car had been stolen from the resident's car park. Eric said, "I've known you for at least five years and I've never seen you drive a car?"

Mary was adamant, "you must have seen me drive it. Don't you remember I drove down from Scotland yesterday?"

Eric thought he better call her son who explained that she did have a car many years ago and was always trying to run off to John O'Groats and in the end they had to take the car away from her.

On another occasion Peggy came down to breakfast the one morning wearing men's clothes. It turned out that Old Joe had forgotten to shut the door to his room and Peggy had wondered in there and put on his clothes over her own outfit that she was currently wearing. When she arrived at the dining room apart from looking twice as big as she normally did, she said, "isn't it hot in here?"

She was escorted back to her own room to change and put Old Joe's clothes back, but Peggy did have the beginning of dementia and had got into the habit of wandering the corridors and going in other people's rooms. Most didn't take much notice and just took her to her own room or one of the communal areas. As with all of the inmates, some days were better than others.

The Matron spoke to Peggy's son and said, "you do realise that your mother has the beginnings of dementia don't you?"

Her son said, "well we know she gets a bit confused but what is it that causes this dementia thing anyway."

"Well, "said the Matron, "we don't really know we think it's something to do with a person's genes."

To which the son replied, "Oh, Mom's never wore jeans and so it can't be that."

Matron just shook her head and said, "never mind, we'll look after her anyway."

Every morning Beryl will say to Priya, "have you seen my wedding ring?" to which Priya would reply, "don't worry Beryl, I'm sure it will turn up." Knowing full well that Beryl had never been married and so does not possess a wedding ring.

One of Eric's trials each morning is to convince Young Joe that he has not lost his shoes but he is actually wearing them. Young Joe was one of the oldest in the Manor and can sometimes get more confused quite a bit some of time. As he's Henry's Dad most of the inmates thinks he knows more than he actually dos. Even if he could remember what he does know it's not really much about what's going on in the Home.

His routine conversation with Eric usually went along the following lines;

Young Joe, "I've lost my shoes."

Eric, "what are they like?"

Young Joe, "well they're like these shoes."

Eric, "like the shoes you have on?"

Young Joe, "yes."

Eric, "well what makes you think they are lost if you are wearing them?"

Young Joe, "oh, you've found them for me, thanks."

Which tended to leave Eric smiling and shaking his head each morning, not knowing if Young Joe was winding him up or not.

The carers help most of the inmates to get up and get washed and dressed and then once the inmates have had breakfast they can go into the communal areas and watch television, or read, or play board games. Most weekdays there are activities which the carers encourage the inmates to take part in. These include keep fit sessions, make-up demonstrations for the ladies, local history talks and other talks on hobbies and activities that the inmates can take part in. It's all very well subscribed, and the inmates consider themselves lucky to have such a dynamic range of activities when compared to similar homes which seem to have lost the will to do anything constructive.

Most of the inmates are fairly placid and go along pretty much with whatever is going on and it's all done in good spirits even when people have what are known as 'senior moments'. The most significant thing is that none of the inmates have lost their zest for life and although they may have slowed down a bit you can still hear them say, "there's life in the old dog yet".

Cyril often remarks, "I'm not as good as I once was, but I'm as good once as ever I was." This has most of the inmates scratching their heads when they hear it not sure exactly what he's trying to say. They usually excuse him by saying, "well, he's an ex-copper, what do you expect?"

There are a few of the more colourful characters who like to bend if not break the rules outright and these particular inmates make life 'interesting' for the rest of the inmates as well as some of the staff at the Manor.

Many of the 'characters' take part in harmless sorts of scams and usually with the help of their family members who visit them. Although a great deal of effort is made trying to keep these extracurricular activities discreet, because of a general difficulty in hearing, a whisper can be heard the other side of the communal areas and so discretion cannot always be maintained.

The betting on the horses is encouraged by the staff as it helps to keep the old brain cells usefully occupied and they also like a bet themselves. Even the buying and selling and the provision of supplies for the Home are encouraged, mainly because it saves money but also because it provides a purpose for some of the inmates and means frequent visits from relatives.

Nearly all of the inmates are making money one way or another. The Home has completely beaten the system in that respect and the extra 'little earners' that the inmates indulge in means everyone's a winner and there's rarely any shortage of cash.

Mo and Priya have their usual tea break, mid-morning, after the inmates have had their breakfast and are settled into whatever routines for the morning. As they know the inmates quite well they sometime stop and have a chat about things.

"Are you looking forward to the Outing Gertie," asks Mo.

"Oh yes, very much so," says Gertie.

"That coach and the driver are the same as last year, what was his name? Denis, Donald – I'm sure it began with the letter D – very superstitious bloke you know," said Mo

Gertie said, "Oh its Derick, his name is Derick. I like to sit by him you know so that I can comfort him. Poor bloke he takes it all very seriously. Still when you've had as many accidents as him you're bound to be a bit nervous."

Mo and Priya looked at each other and Priya said, "I always thought he was a bit erratic as a driver but didn't realise he'd had a lot of accidents?"

"Oh yes," said Gertie, "he was telling me all about it at the last outing." She paused for effect and then said, "you do know that I have the gift don't you?"

"What gift's that Gertie then?" said Mo.

"You know the gift, tea leaves and all that," replied Gertie.

Mo and Priya said together, "you mean you read tea leaves?"

"Exactly," said Gertie, "give me your cups and I'll let you know what Friday has in store for you two."

So Mo and Priya hand over their cups and Gertie looks at one and then the other doing a lot of oohing and ahhing as she does so.

"I can tell you both now that you are going to have a good time on Friday. The tea leaves indicate a slightly unusual outing for you but nothing to worry about. It looks like you'll both be going off on your own perhaps with a smaller group somewhere," prophesised Gertie.

"That sounds rather intriguing doesn't it, Mo?" said Priya.

"I'm just looking forward to a day out, me, that'll be a bit of a break in itself," replied Mo as they both went off to carry out the rest of their duties.

Bert and the General had overheard Gertie's predictions and a discussion on superstitions ensued.

"Superstitions! That's all they are," said the General.

"Don't you mock now General," said Gertie, "there's many a thing we don't understand. What is that they say – 'there are more things in heaven and Earth' – so it's best to keep an open mind."

"Well what are we talking about here Gertie," asked Bert, "I mean you can't really see the future, can you?"

"There's all sorts of things dear," replied Gertie, "I mean let's just take your basic superstitions. All of them have got a good reason for people to be wary of them. Take walking under a ladder, for example, everyone knows it's best not to in case something falls on your head. But did you know that the superstition dates back to ancient Egypt? Oh yes, the Egyptians thought that the shape of the triangle, formed by leaning a ladder against a wall will break the power of the pyramid, which is where the triangle shape came from, and so result in really bad luck."

The General said, "I think it's a load of old bol……. toffee if you ask me.

"I'm not so sure General, you carry on Gertie," said Bert.

Gertie was getting into her stride and went into full flow about the whys and wherefores of superstitions some which Bert and the General thought she'd made up.

"Of course a lot depends on interpretation which is where my particular gift comes in. I'm able to read the signs see? You know if you see a black cat to some people it can be unlucky and yet others say that if a black cat crosses your path you will have good luck. Black cats got a lot of bad press when they became associated with witches but again this goes back to the ancient Egyptians who used to worship cats. Also we have superstitions is this country which are different in other countries, like the number seven, we think it's a lucky number but that's not the case in China. We don't really know why seven is supposed to be lucky. It might be something to do with 'seventh heaven' or because initially it was thought there were only seven planets."

Bert was nodding his head as though it all made sense but the General was looking sceptical.

Gertie went on about full moons, spilling salt and four-leaf clovers which Bert and the General both picked up on as they both firmly believed in luck because of betting on the horses when sometimes you needed a bit of luck as well as studying form.

"But what does it all mean – luck that is – can you even have good luck and bad luck?" asked Bert.

"Well there's certainly bad luck. You only have to look at some of the horses we've backed to know that a horse doesn't always romp home first," said the General, "even when it's a cast iron certainty."

Gertie said, "but you know, some people are naturally lucky, aren't they? How do you think that happens then and can you make your own luck? There are a lot of books about nowadays, telling people to 'think lucky, and they'll be lucky', and perhaps it's just as simple as that."

"Well it's been my experience that you can get naturally lucky and naturally unlucky people," said Bert, "and to paraphrase that golfer – 'the harder you work the luckier you get'. So I don't think luck exists on its own and I do think you need to work at it to get lucky."

"Luck's a bit like willpower – there's only so much of it to go around –this is why so many people fall off the wagon when they are trying to give up the booze or whatever other addictions they have. There just isn't enough willpower and likewise there just isn't enough luck," replied the General.

Gertie said, "well so long as there's enough luck for us lot at Redcar on Friday that's all we'll need for now."

"Can't you see the future Gertie?" asked Bert, "I mean the tea leaves an' all isn't that about predicting the future? I know some people have used things like Ouija boards."

Gertie looked a bit askance at Bert and said, "where did you come up with that idea. There are clairvoyants and such like who are supposed to predict the future by consulting with the spirit world……."

"The only spirits I'm interested in is in my hip flask," interrupted the General.

"And I'm not so sure it's such a good idea to disturb those things that we don't know much about," concluded Gertie.

"It reminds me of a time that Cyril and Old Joe went ghost hunting," began the General, "they heard that one of the rooms at the very top of the house was haunted. I forget who told them now but whoever it was pretty convincing. So the one night Cyril and Old Joe decided to go in search of this ghost and so they crept up the stairs to the room which I think is the one at the very top in the corner."

Bert and Gertie were both on the edge of their seats and Bert said, "well, what happened?"

The General continued, "they located the room alright and it was just coming up to midnight. So Cyril, quiet as he could, slowly opened the door, just a bit, so they could look in. Well Old Joe was behind him and the next thing he knows is Cyril flying past him and hurtling down the stairs at some speed. So Old Joe hightails it after him asking, 'what is it Cyril, what did you see? Was it a ghost?' Cyril caught his breath and says 'just as I opened the door Mo came out of the bathroom with nothing on and I could just see us coming up in front of a judge saying that we were just looking for ghosts as a defence for being peeping Toms'."

The General guffawed with laughter and Bert and Gertie let out the breaths they had been holding and laughed as well.

"That's a very funny story General," said Gertie and she and Bert walked away still smiling. She said, "wait till I see Cyril or Old Joe, I shall play them up about this now."

The General went in search of something to refill his hip flask. Now that he'd mentioned it he was reminded that he needed to get it refilled ready for the outing on Friday.

CHAPTER 6

Private Enterprise is alive and well and living at the Manor

"It's getting more like a retirement home for people who sail close to the wind," said Leeroy whilst he was on his mid-morning break.

Burnt Offering replied, "are you going to sit there all day? I need you to help me with the lunches today because we've got some visitors."

Leeroy said, "well I'm only just saying about all the deals and fiddles going on in the Manor here makes it look about as bent as the City of London on steroids. Anyway, I thought Sharon was helping you?"

"And what would you know about the City of London, Leeroy? You've never been anywhere other than Piccadilly Circus when you've been on a day trip into London town. Sharon needs to help Eric with the inmates today because of the visitors coming and so you're helping with the lunches."

"What visitors are these?" asked Leeroy.

Burnt Offering shook his head and said, "I don't really know, but I think it's something to do with the Council or Social Services. You know we get grants from these organisations and the government like to make sure the money is well spent."

"Oh," said Leeroy, "best of luck to them provided that's all they want to do and that they don't look too closely at some of the other activities the inmates get up to. There's enough going on in this Home to support the entire British economy single handed." He went on to explain this exaggeration as he helped Burnt Offering prepare the dinner for lunch time complaining that he was nothing short of being a 'dogsbody round here'. He said, exaggerating, "not only do I have to help the inmates, but I also have to deal with all the buying and selling admin as well as look after supplies and stores."

Burnt Offering said, "not my stores, you don't, I look after them personally. Anyway they've given you the job title of Stores Manager, haven't they and I thought Betty dealt with all the admin?"

Leeroy just shrugged his shoulders but did reluctantly confirm that he did indeed have such a job title but there was precious little extra in his pay packet to indicate that that had happened. He said, "what I really need is to get in on some of the scams the management and inmates are working on and then I can make a few quid extra."

Burnt Offering just shook his head and said, "well let's get the dinner served first before you become a business tycoon."

The inmates and the staff preferred to have their main dinner during the day at lunchtime and then just a sandwich at dinner time, which they called teatime, although some referred to it as supper time because it was just before everything wrapped up for the night. It could be a bit confusing for newcomers not knowing if they were having their dinner or their lunch, but Burnt Offering managed to finish early by cooking dinner at lunch time rather than teatime.

When Gertie tried to explain this to a newcomer the once the lady got so confused and so Gertie said, "just think of the old saying about breakfasting like a king, lunching like a price and dining like a pauper, that some people live by."

To which the new lady had replied will that help me remember if I'm having lunch or dinner?"

"Not really dear, "Gertie had said, "but it's a nice saying anyway."

Leeroy continued, "I know you look after your own stores and that you've got a nice little system worked out haven't you? I mean everyone in this place seems to be fiddling everybody else. There's Gertie and that grandson of hers, Terry, who can get you anything if the price is right. Gertie's also into that betting syndicate that Harry, the General and Bert take part in. Then there's Elizabeth and her stock market fiddle that she works with her granddaughter. They're never short of a few bob that pair, that's for sure, and she gets the Financial Times each week to convince the other inmates that she's a 'player' and so can work other scams on them. I'm not kidding you, it's like the Wild West in that community room sometimes."

Burnt Offering was doing very nicely thank you and so kept quiet about the various 'extracurricular activities' he was working on. All he knew was that his retirement fund was looking very healthy – thank you very much.

Burnt Offering hailed from Scotland and looked a little bit like the wrestler from a few years back called Giant Haystacks. He was a very tall, large bloke with long red hair and a busy red beard. When he gets angry no one can understand him as he reverts to his native Glaswegian accent which is more of a dialect in its own right rather than a massive mispronunciation of the English language.

Having said this he is surprisingly quite a good cook having trained at various London Hotels. He actually started at the Savoy and gradually worked his way down from there as each establishment suffered under his anger management issues.

So although he never actually finished any of the posh hotel training courses he did however pick up enough to be a passably good cook or chef as he likes to be called. The last person who called him a cook should be leaving hospital any time soon.

The 'Burnt Offering' moniker came about because he was actually preparing breakfast one day on his own and he'd burnt the toast. This had almost set fire to the kitchen and there was an all-pervasive burnt smell for days to come.

His real name is Tony, and he takes his nickname as a good sport provided it's not said in malice. People have learned the hard way not to ever get on the wrong side of him as his temper is legendary. He would even make Gordon Ramsay blush with some of the words he can come out with.

Tony, as he was then known, specialised as a pastry chef and made some remarkable dessert creations. He could make really good puddings, sweets, desserts and cakes and, as he used to like to sample his 'creations' he became known as Tony Two Cakes in those days because in his enthusiasm he could never just eat one cake.

Having not only lost his temper but had more like a vitriolic meltdown at the last hotel he was with he'd ended up at the Manor and in actual fact this environment suited him better than the rather regimented hotel set up. So he'd actually thrived and the people who eat his dinners and sweet creations were very appreciative. Although praise was offered sparingly in case it was taken the wrong way and set him off on one of his red mist rants.

As the General also hailed from Scotland, he and Burnt Offering occasionally converse with one another but there is a fundamental problem; Burnt Offering is from the notorious Gorbals area of Glasgow and so almost by definition supports the Celtic football team and the General comes from one of the more refined areas and so obviously support Rangers. They are therefore very wary of each other. On one occasion when Celtic had won against Rangers there had been an almighty row between the two of them. Each had gone back over the years quoting various statistics as to why their team was better than the other. This had escalated to the point where Burnt Offering had almost taken a saucepan to the General's head, which would have done him no good at all. Fortunately Eric had been passing by at the time and had managed to intervene thus avoiding Burnt Offering coming up on a murder charge. Those inmates that witnessed the exchange between the General and Burnt Offering are still not sure to this day what the fuss was about because of the reversion to broad Scottish accents meant that only about one word in ten could be understood.

Leeroy took Burnt Offering's silence as agreement and spouted on "You know Young Joe sons' the accountant for the home don't you? You can't tell me that him and Ajay aren't pulling a few strokes. I mean most care homes are just about managing, 'hand to mouth', so to speak, but here we are, got everything we need, we're all on a relatively good 'bung' and we have trips and all sorts. The money's got to come from somewhere, hasn't it?"

"Well whatever you do, don't mention it to Cyril because he used to be a copper you know. He's always on about arresting people and his granddaughter is in the police force now as well. It's a good job he gets a bit mixed up, from time to time, and thinks his still on the job but you never know what he's telling that granddaughter of his or who else he might be talking to or what contacts he has back on the force," said Burnt Offering.

"It's service now, not force, they don't like to call it police force because it smacks too much of state control," pointed out Leeroy.

"Hark at you, force, service, what's the difference they'll still give you a clout and lock you up if they catch you."

"Ah that's exactly it isn't it – if they catch you. There's really only one rule you know?"

"What's that then?" asked Burnt Offering

Leeroy concluded, "don't get caught!"

Leeroy continued on about making some easy money and Burnt Offering hadn't the heart to tell him about the latest investment scheme that Ajay and Henry were about to launch. Burnt Offering was thinking that he'd get in first and that his retirement fund would be looking even better soon. However Leeroy did manage to approach the subject of the investment scheme with Ajay and was asked if he would be interested in the administration of the scheme which would mean a nice little earner for him and so naturally he jumped at the chance.

They need not have worried too much about Cyril even though he did try to arrest people at the drop of a hat. He just got a bit confused having been with the police for such a long time. But these days he was more likely to be a 'poacher' rather than a 'gamekeeper', as it were.

Cyril was another one of the constant talkers and could talk at length about anything and everything to the point of sometimes boring the other inmates to sleep. However he did have a fund of jokes which kept most people on their toes.

One of his most popular jokes, that he never tired of telling, was that he went to the doctors the other day and told him he was going to marry a nineteen year old girl. The doctor looked him over and said it could be dangerous to which he replied – "well if she dies, she dies."

Cyril liked a drink more than most and his main preoccupation was funding the rather expensive red wines that he liked. With the help of Eric, the head carer, they managed to work a 'flanker' on the 'poncey wine clubs' that he called them. There were usually vouchers and offers to get a case or two here and there and with a bit of manoeuvring Eric and Cyril managed to get what they wanted without parting with too much cash. Betty always managed to 'sub' them anyway and so most evenings Eric, Cyril and Harry would have a drink or two together. Both the General and Bert used to join in but they preferred whisky really. Most of the women meanwhile had managed to secure their own supply of gin and tonic. There always seemed to be enough booze about and there was a good stock of beers, wines and spirits at any given time.

Old Joe, being one of the youngest in the Home, could still legitimately (if it's possible to use that word in such an environment) go to work as he was only just about past retirement age. In fact Old Joe had retired several times but managed to get himself hired again on a day rate basis. He did this so often that he became known as the 'Comeback Kid' because he might disappear for a few weeks and then he'd be back at the Home. Although it was repeatedly pointed out to him that the Manor wasn't a hotel but was supposed to be an older persons retirement home he just kept saying that that was the last time and that now he he'd retired for good.

One of the advantages for Old Joe in still doing a bit of work for various organisations was that he'd built up quite a network of contacts mainly in the Events Industry and so he could get tickets for shows, plays, exhibitions and other live events. There was never any charge other than a 'drink' for whoever was getting the tickets. The major difficulty was in sneaking out of a night although one of the inmates, Tom Baxter, known as Soups Baxter or just Soups, could always arrange transportation even though he might moan about it somewhat. Soups was a really good fixer and could organise most things. It helped that he was a master forger as well and so any documents, tickets or passes required he could produce, and they always looked pretty authentic. He could be a bit of a misery on occasion because he was kept so busy but generally if he was asked nicely he'd deliver what was required.

Peggy was saying to Mary, "I don't know what I'd do if we didn't get all those discounts off the clothes and the makeup and the like. That grandson of Gertie's a Godsend, what's his name again?" Both Mary and Peggy were what were considered to be well preserved even if they couldn't remember names.

Mary said, "well I think standards have to be maintained, don't you Peggy?"

She went on, "it's all very well being comfortable but if you look at the state of some of these women. I mean they look like tramps. Breeding of course helps. You've only got to look at Gertie to realise that. A right toff and no mistake."

"Unlike us though, eh?" said Peggy. Peggy came from a large family of brothers and sisters, sons and daughters and now grandchildren. She'd never been particularly well off but with all the scams being worked at the Manor she had discovered, like Mary, that you could indeed live very well for very much less there.

Peggy went on, "I do know what you mean though, just because someone was brought up on the 'other side of the tracks' as they used to say, doesn't mean that they can't make an effort to better themselves though, does it?"

"Well you know what I always say Peggy," said Mary, "and that's clothes maketh the man… and the woman!"

"Quite!" said Peggy, "I mean these days people don't seem to care about their appearance. Men and women both! You see men who have not shaved for days on end, and women wearing something like what the cat might have brought in. Some of them don't even have the figure to pull it off and it makes them look a right old state."

Mary was nodding and said, "I know exactly what you mean. You see some of them with their midriff showing and about ten pounds of ugly fat bulging out! It's these torn jeans that get me. My husband used to have a pair like that which he used to do the decorating in – now the youngsters would pay a fortune to have a pair of jeans like that! – I just don't get it."

"Some of the clothes just look like underwear to me and the tattoos some of them have, what's that all about then? I don't get it, I really don't. Some of the youngsters today have their whole arm or leg or both arms and both legs tattooed to the point where you can hardly see any gaps of flesh. It's gotta hurt hasn't it?" said Peggy.

"You and I both come from a far more glamorous era where sartorial elegance was the order of the day," Mary went on, "these days they throw anything on even if it doesn't co-ordinate. Do you remember when the greatest insult was to call a woman 'common'? Well the younger ones wouldn't have a clue what you meant now. They're as common as S.H.1.T! if you will forgive my French."

Conversations like this between the inmates tended to be viewed behind rose tinted glasses and nostalgia usually got the better of the inmates although occasionally something profound could be heard, especially if you kept your ears open. Quite frequently someone would remark that nostalgia isn't what it used to be! This could be then repeated throughout the day as the inmates tended to forget who first said or indeed if they'd said it all.

In spite of all of the scams and private enterprise activities there was never any stealing amongst the inmates. There was an occasion once where Sharon had lost her watch and thought one of the inmates might have taken it. It turned out that there was a relatively younger man, who looked to be about the same age as Old Joe who had a tendency to 'borrow' things. His name was Kevin and whenever he went out anywhere he would bring back 'souvenirs' of one sort or another. The staff and inmates had nicknamed him as Kevin the Klepto and he was asked if he would mind if his room was searched when the watch went missing. Kevin, being a very placid bloke who didn't really realise what he was doing had no objection and it turned out to be like an Aladdin's Cave. There were all sorts of sweets and chocolate bars, mostly past their sell by date, packets of crisps, cakes and biscuits also way past their best before dates. He had all sorts of over the counter medicinal remedies that he must have acquired from chemist shops and so on. But there was no watch and so Sharon was asked to run through the last time she remembered wearing it. Sharon thought so long and hard that it was painful to see her trying to recall her earlier movements – there was almost steam coming out of her ears. Eventually she realised that she had taken her watch off to help Burnt Offering in the kitchen and mistakenly put it in the fridge!

The discovery about Kevin was a bit alarming and Nurse Brown had a chat with him to see if she could find out more about this tendency of his to take things particularly as they would have liked to return what they could have. However Kevin wasn't very forthcoming and so it was 'brushed under the carpet' basically as the staff didn't really want to worry the rest of the inmates and they considered it to be a harmless 'pastime' for him.

Peggy's granddaughter was called Debbie, so as not to be confused with other's granddaughters called Deborah. It seemed that the inmate's grandsons and granddaughters all had fairly common names which did not help one bit when one of them referred to a particular grandson or granddaughter by the incorrect name. Life was confusing enough as it was and having a number of visiting relatives appear all with the same name could be a bit of a nightmare.

This particular Debbie though could supply medical treatments and equipment. She worked for one of the big pharmaceutical companies and was forever bringing in samples of new lines. She could also access prescription drugs and so if Matron was being a bit stingy with medication, then an order went out to Debbie to get some in.

Debbie would bring in a new line to help with some minor ailment or other and she would say something like, "these are fantastic. You won't feel a thing and they are totally non-addictive – I take them all the time!"

Debbie, visited Peggy at least once a week and always had the latest orders with her. These, of course, had to be smuggled in, because Nurse Brown and the Matron would have had the proverbial fit, which would be equivalent to the Last Judgement updated to include lasers and cannon, if they'd found out.

Quite frequently these illicit supplies would have to be hidden in the community room somewhere, especially if Matron or the Nurse approached. This could be quite hazardous because if Kevin the Klepto was about he would pick them up and stash them in his room even though he wasn't particularly on any medication himself – he just liked taking things, and he liked the brightly coloured packaging with all the warnings about taking prototype medicines.

As Debbie arrived the inmates would line up in the community room to receive their ill-gotten supplies. Debbie had asked Peggy to do something about that because it looked like the inmates were waiting for a drugs 'pusher'. Peggy said, "it's just that they're pleased to see you, that's all." Usually a few pounds changed hands and Peggy and Betty the bookkeeper would deal with the finances. Each individual had their own account and it was not only financial matters recorded there. Included within Betty's 'system' was also an exchange rate bartering arrangement where the valuation of items bartered was subject to free market economics and basic salesmanship. Since nearly everyone had additional income sources then there was never an issue with either unpaid bills or un-swapped barters.

Gertie's grandson Terry was a bit like a market trader and could get literally anything any time providing there was sufficient profit in it for him. Very often there would be conversations along the lines, "do you need any shirts, Bert?" he would ask.

To which Bert would reply, "I can get my shirts for free Terry from Old Joe."

Terry would think about this for a short time and after pondering the dilemma announce that he couldn't beat that price and move on to ask someone else.

"Well somebody's got to keep the economy going," Betty was saying to Elizabeth.

"You can't trust something as important as that to the government. Anyway they all operate a 'wheels within wheels' policy as well, don't they? Those government ministers and even prime ministers have all lined their own pockets and so you might say that we're all following in a fine old British tradition."

Betty carried on, "I was only saying to Henry the other day, you know Henry dear don't you? He's Young Joe's son. Such a nice lad. Qualified accountant you know and he and I get on like a house on fire."

"Don't you worry about the balloon ever going up? You know someone blowing the whistle on you?" asked Elizabeth.

"What do you mean dear? It's all accounted for, in what Henry describes as the most secure book-keeping system he's ever seen. Esoteric he calls it, such a nice man," said Betty.

Elizabeth continued, "it seems to me that there's a few people in here, staff and inmates, who, shall we say, cut a few corners to be polite."

"Well everyone tends to have their own particular interests," admitted Betty, "still it keeps them out of mischief though doesn't it?"

To which Elizabeth just shook her head and thought that she needed to talk to her granddaughter, Rebecca, about their next share buying scheme. She tended to rationalise that what she and Rebecca did helped the economy even though they didn't pay any tax these days. She considered that what the other inmates was up to was a bit 'vulgar' even though it all helped keep the Manor well stocked and well-funded.

Leeroy, Eric, Sharon, Mo and Pryia were all having an afternoon tea break. It should be staggered really but Leeroy and Sharon were about to go off to help out elsewhere when Eric and the other two carers arrived in the dining room.

Leeroy started on again about the activities going on in the community room. He said, "I've just been watching them all and do you know that every last one of them has got some sort of fiddle or scam going on. It's unbelievable!"

Sharon, not being the brightest of the carers said, "well I think it's nice that they have some interesting things to be doing at their age, don't you Eric"

Eric pondered for a few seconds and said, "well, I suppose, there's different ways of looking at it. On the one had it does give the inmates something to do, something they can look forward to and it also helps out with their finances as well."

"But?" said Leeroy jumping in.

"How do you know if there is a 'but'?" said Eric.

"It's just the way you built it up and I'm just expecting you to knock it down again," Leeroy explained.

Eric looked at him and said, "no it's not that Leeroy, it's just that they sail too close to the wind for my liking and if they ever do get 'rumbled' then who knows what might happen and not only to them but to all of us. What if they closed the place down?"

"Oh they wouldn't do that," said Sharon.

"Why not?" said Eric, "we've got a bunch of do-gooders from Social Services and the Council who are coming in tomorrow morning and God knows what they'll think of the place!"

"Well we'd all be out of jobs, wouldn't we?" replied Sharon.

"Yeah?" said Leeroy as Eric just gave that look of his that made them wonder if they were right.

"Well they wouldn't, would they Eric?" Sharon said exasperatedly.

Eric went on, "I don't know what would happen, but I do know that while it's going well we might as well leave well alone." Which confused everybody and he went on, "these shall we say, 'activities' keep them happy as well and I'm sure that it certainly keeps the old brain cells working and so dementia's being kept at bay for most of them because of all these goings on, at least it's not as serious as it could be. We'll just have to wait and see if there's any fallout from the visitors tomorrow. I wish Burn…. Tony… hadn't gone to town on the lunch he'll be serving up for them though, it sort of gives the game away!"

CHAPTER 7

The Visitors

Ajay and Brenda had welcomed the visitors from the Local Authority Council and Social Services in his office. There was also some government official carrying out a study on old people's homes who had a tagged along and so there were seven of these fairly officious looking individuals. All of them seemed to have a frown on their faces and Ajay said to Brenda, "we might need some reinforcements, let's get Betty in as well and tell Sharon to break out the chocolate biscuits."

Fortunately there was a meeting room adjacent to Ajay's office which could accommodate them all. The seven sat one side of the table and Ajay, Brenda and Betty on the other side each looking somewhat concerned about the other side.

A rather large woman called Miranda Fortescue-Barton started. She was wearing a tweed two piece and a single row of pearls and looked like a throwback to the 1950s. She seemed to be in charge and was something to do with the Council. A formidable woman who had a perpetual frown and an expression as though she had just swallowed a wasp. She obviously tolerated no nonsense and tended to shout to disguise the fact that she was hard of hearing. Ajay wondered if it was too late to call Matron in – she'd be a match for this woman who was beginning to scare him and they hadn't even got going yet.

"I won't beat about the bush Mr Ajay we….." she began.

"It's not Mr Ajay," said Ajay, "it's either Ajay or Mr Chowdhury, I don't mind....."

"Whatever," Fortescue-Barton interrupted, "you can call me FB if you like, most people do. I should just introduce the others before we go any further I suppose."

The Local Authority Council contingent consisted of Miranda Fortescue-Barton, or FB as she liked to be called, a Mr Cecil Humphries and a Mr Sadiq Khan. All of them looked to be typical bureaucrats who slavishly followed the rules with a 'jobsworth' mentality and the imagination of a brick.

FB turned to the rather grey looking man on her right and said, "perhaps you would like to introduce yourself and your associates from Social Services, Mr Piper?"

Mr Piper was a short slight man that looked like a strong gust of wind would blow him over. Sitting next to Miranda Fortescue-Barton they looked like little and large version of a bureaucratic template.

He said, "My name's Peter Piper, I know, I've heard it all before, so just call me Peter. This is my associate Indira Banerjee and on my far right is Ms Stella Standish who is our LBGT representative."

Ajay, Brenda and Betty nodded and mumbled some "pleased to meet you's". They were a bit puzzled as to why they needed so many people for this visit and especially specialist busy bodies representing things like LGBT.

"Oh, and I should just add that the gentleman at the end there is Mr Leonard Baptiste who is from central government who is carrying out a study on old people's homes as part of a government, think tank initiative."

There were so many contradictions with the words government, think and initiative that it was unbelievable that someone could come out with such an introduction thought Ajay.

"Shall I get Sharon to bring us some coffee before we start so that we're not interrupted?" asked Ajay, "I could also get Matron to join us as I think she will provide some valuable input," Ajay bluffed.

"No, I don't think so, not just yet" FB jumped in before anyone else could express an opinion. "I would like to get started straightaway with the very serious issues that have come to our attention!"

Ajay, Brenda and Betty just stared at her with mouths wide open wondering what 'serious issues' she was talking about.

FB went on, "it has come to light that the latest grants provided to you have all gone and been spent, as we understand it, already. This was a considerable sum of money and we would like to know what you have done with it all!" she shouted.

"Come to light?" said Brenda, "I didn't know it was in the dark. We have always been very transparent about our dealings with the Local Authority, haven't we Betty?"

Betty picked up the baton and said, "Oh yes, very transparent indeed. Everything is accounted for and meticulously recorded in our system so there's nothing 'in the dark' about it." she smiled at FB who scowled back.

Peter Piper piped up and said rather sheepishly, "it's just that it's all gone quite quickly and we would like to know what it has been spent on if that's alright with you. We have your new application for a further grant and it just seemed to us that you are obtaining grants when you shouldn't really need them"

"We want a full accounting immediately!" shouted FB who wasn't taking any prisoners. She looked at Peter Piper and shook her head thinking the most aggressive he is ever likely to get would be the equivalent of being savaged by a dead sheep.

Ajay said, "Betty perhaps you could show these people the accounts including the disbursement of the grants and explain how we use the money here?"

"Certainly," said Betty, "I'll just go and get my ledger. Could somebody give me hand please? It is rather heavy and it usually remains in my office area because it's difficult to move."

Sadiq and Stella offered to help and came back carrying Betty's ledger as you would a small table, both struggling to get it through the door of the meeting room. Stella, who was into body building, didn't seem to notice but Sadiq said that it was heavy to which Indira made some derogatory comment under her breath. There was clearly a lot of animosity there thought Ajay.

Brenda turned the ledger, which took up most of the surface of the table, to face the visitors and Betty started going through the various entries. Pretty soon the visitor's eyes started to glaze over until FB shouted, "Enough! This is getting us nowhere!"

Betty stopped what she was saying and looked at FB and then the others. Brenda and Ajay were just about to say something when Cecil and Stella started a discussion about the activities at the Home.

Stella said, "it looks to me like this Home treats everyone the same."

"Quite so, and I wonder how the various minorities get on," added Cecil.

Brenda said, "I'm not sure what you're getting at. Everyone is treated the same including ethnic minorities."

"No we don't mean that," said Stella, "what about the LBGT community?"

"What LBGT community is this?" said Ajay.

Cecil and Stella looked at each other and rounded on Ajay, "you must have some gays and/or lesbians here at least. The age of your residents makes the transgender issues unlikely. But we want to know how you look after the LGB people separately!" said Stella rather forcefully.

Brenda chipped in, "I dare say one or two residents may have had, let's say 'tendencies' in the past, but everyone is treated the same here – regardless of their tendencies – so we would not treat them 'separately' in any way."

THE OUTING

Cecil said, "I don' think that's good enough they need to be regarded as special cases."

Betty was happy for the discussion to carry on in this vein and said nothing but Ajay and Brenda both thought that treating anyone any differently to other people was a silly idea and Ajay said, "perhaps we should get some of the inmates, I mean residents, in here to talk to you. Get their views sort of thing?"

There were nods all around the table and so Ajay said to Brenda, "could you go and see if you can find the General, Bert and Cyril, and ask them if they could join us?"

FB was quick off the mark saying that they would also need to talk to female residents as well as the men and Ajay confirmed that that would be arranged later.

The General, who was so right wing he thought of Attila the Hun as a liberal, led the three of them into the meeting room and said, "what's all this then Ajay, been caught fiddling the books?" and laughed much to Betty's discomfort.

FB welcomed them to the meeting even though it was in the Home's meeting room. She said, "we would like your views on a couple of matters and do please be honest about what you think so that we can assess how well this Home meets requirements."

Bert and Cyril both sat down next to Brenda and looked expectantly at FB who proceeded to explain in no uncertain terms that they were here to make sure that the grants provided to the Manor were used for legitimate purposes and that they now wanted their views of the treatment of the LBGT community at the Home.

The General, Bert and Cyril were initially speechless and the General said with all the dignity he could muster, "I don't think you'll find any 'shirt-lifters' here dear."

FB was outraged not only because of the use of the word 'dear' but referring to gay people as 'shirt-lifters' she spluttered, "that's an outrageous thing to say!"

"No it's true, dear, I can assure you," continued the General, completely oblivious to the potential volcanic nature of FB's temper, "there are one or two that are a bit girly, like that Kevin chappie, but on the whole the men are men here isn't that right?" looking at Bert and Cyril.

Bert and Cyril both nodded in agreement which was a bit unusual for them as generally they could not agree with each other on any matter whatsoever. But they did so now however find themselves in total agreement.

Cyril said, "this is all getting out of hand these days; LBGT, WOKE, whatever that stands for. It's all 'tail wagging the dog', in my days on the force, when I first started, it was illegal anyway."

Bert added, "I don't think anyone minds what a person's gender or sexual orientation is and that's up to them. The General's terminology was a bit unfortunate but that's just a generation thing. What I, and others, don't like is it being thrust under your noses all the while. Let people get on with whatever they want to but don't think that you need to parade it round because basically most people have enough worries of their own without needing constant reminding about other people's tendencies."

"Quite right," confirmed the General, "no one has the right to interfere with another's viewpoint and we have our own views which are no doubt different to yours but that doesn't make them any less relevant. Just because we may not agree with parading around and shouting about certain things it does not mean to say that our view is any less valid."

Cyril added, "we're supposed to have freedom of speech in this country but these days everyone has to be so careful about what they say because they might offend someone. If the arguments are strong enough then they will stand up to debate. We don't need this 'thought police' approach. People need to toughen up a bit if they get offended at the slightest un-PC comment!"

FB, Stella and Cecil were beside themselves and all three had gone a funny shade of purple. "How dare you!" shouted FB, "I've a good mind to report you to the police for a hate crime!"

"Now let's not be hasty," said Ajay, "you wanted their views and you asked them to be honest and now just because you don't like the answers they've given you want to throw your toys out of the pram! The General, Bert and Cyril are of a certain generation when they could say basically whatever they liked even though it may have offended some people. I know these days that such words and statements are no longer tolerated but we did ask for their honest opinion."

The General was on his feet and fixed FB with a rigid stare. He said, "madam, we did not ask you here, and please keep in mind that you are a visitor in our Home, to which we extend all common courtesy, but don't think you can bully us into your way of thinking. We are all individuals here and we have the right to think our own thoughts without having someone else's view shoved down our throats. The problem with this country today is that it places so little store on the individual and the tremendous amount of human potential that each of us possess. No, these days it's committees this and committees that. Let me tell you that the definition of a committee is.... it's where decision go to die!"

"It's individuals that make the difference," he went on, "between the mediocre and the excellent. The self-reliance and willing to accept individual responsibility whilst having due consideration for other people that is what makes for greatness. And having the backbone to stand up for what is right even though the pressure against you may be very great indeed. It's not petty minded bureaucrats who slavishly follow the rules in a jobsworth manner that matter. It's individuals who stand on their own two feet and face up to their responsibilities and have the right to be able to think freely. Individuals need to be individuals in order to achieve great things!"

Bert and Cyril started clapping and then Ajay, Brenda and Betty joined them. The Local Authority and Social Services people just gave off menacing stares whilst Leonard was scribbling furiously into his notebook.

Cyril said, "I agree wholeheartedly with the General and couldn't have put it better myself."

"What people must realise," added Bert is that organisations are there to serve people – and the people who work in them also need to realise that – you should not bend the will of the individual to suit the organisation. No that wouldn't be right at all! As Albert Einstein once said 'we cannot solve our problems with the same thinking we used when we created them', and I do believe these past few years have created more than enough problems!"

FB was fuming and was just about to retaliate when Leonard Baptiste said, "haven't we strayed from our remit a bit here?" Peter Piper and Indira Banerjee both nodded their heads and Sadiq said, "that's right, we're supposed to be assessing if the grants are being used wisely not debating the rights of the individual and these wider issues."

FB said, "well judging by what we've just heard I don't think the grants are being used in the right way at all!"

Brenda jumped in and replied, "what on Earth has a person's personal view of things got to do with how the Home is being run?"

"They shouldn't be thinking that way," said Stella, "it's just not right." Stella's initials were SS and as she worked for Social Services, or SS for short, it was frequently remarked by people who had come across her that SS from the SS was every bit as mean, menacing and cantankerous as her initials would indicate.

"Their personal views are just that – personal, and have nothing whatsoever to do with the running of this Home," stated Ajay fixing the visitors with a hard stare.

The discussion continued on the use of the grants and Betty again managed to confuse everyone with her 'system' and when none of the visitors could think of any other questions to ask Stella said, "I think we would like to hear from the female residents now."

"Well OK," said FB, "but I have to say that I've had bowel movements lasting longer than some of these grants that you've spent. I don't think I've ever seen money disappear so quickly and I think we shall need to have another look at this Outing thing that's planned for later this week."

Ajay said, "by all means we can return to the Outing after you have interviewed the female inmates."

Elizabeth, Gertie, Beryl and Peggy all arrived together with some coffee and biscuits. Ajay had made sure that Sharon knew to provide the best chocolate biscuits that Home had, and plenty of them to "try and 'sweeten' this lot up."

After the introductions were made FB asked the female inmates what they thought of how the Home was run and Elizabeth kicked off by saying that she thought it was wonderful.

Gertie added, "this is really like a 'Home from Home' as it were, and the staff and all the other inmates are friendly and generally get on well with one another. I wasn't too sure at first you know? When I first moved in that is. But after a few weeks I soon settled down and now I'm so pleased that I live here. We all get on very well together and we have lots of activities. We've got the Outing coming up on Friday and did you know......"

"That's quite enough thank you very much, Mrs.. Mrs.... Gertie or whatever your name is," jumped in FB, "we have a lot to cover and so need to move on!"

"It's interesting you call the residents here inmates," said Peter Piper. To which Beryl replied, "is that really your name only we know a tongue twister about a Peter Piper?"

FB interrupted and said, "there's no need to be insulting about Peter's name!"

Beryl said, "Oh, I didn't mean anything by it dear, I was just saying….."

"Can we please get on," said Peter getting somewhat flustered, "why do the residents call themselves inmates. Is it because it's like a prison?"

"It's a joke," said Elizabeth, "surely you remember what one of those are?"

Peggy added, "I think I can speak for all of us by saying that this Home encourages us to keep active and have a variety of interests. We are respected as individuals and most importantly were are treated like human beings!"

"Here, Here," said Gertie, "I wholeheartedly concur with Peggy!" Beryl and Elizabeth both nodded vigorously to also show their support for Peggy's comments.

FB and the other visitors gave a weapons grade look of disgust whilst Ajay, Brenda and Betty were smiling. Ajay said, "I think we've covered everything Mrs FB and……"

"It's just FB is you please not Mrs FB," said FB interrupting angrily, "I'm not so sure we should leave it there as there are still a numbered of unanswered questions which….."

Gertie jumped in and said, "I would like to conclude by saying that we need to consider the human condition far more than just discussing how the Home operates. You need to understand what makes people happy."

She then launched into her philosophy of life saying, "it doesn't really take a lot to make people happy. A bit of food and drink and some music. People generally like to have a sing song and perhaps a bit of dancing if they're up to it.

Socialising with family and friends especially when it's a special occasion like a birthday or an anniversary. At one stage Christmas and to a lesser extent other holidays, like Easter, used to be good fun and made people happy but these days greed's took over. It's no longer what can I do for you but all you hear is I want…want….want… want, that seems that's all that people are interested in – themselves!

And do you know it's a fallacy that having 'things' makes you happy. Initially as new things became available we all thought how wonderful they were – the Hoover, washing machines, dish washers and of course the telly and that.

But technology's gone made, hasn't it. It's a bit like what they used to say about fire and water – they make good servants but very bad masters. Technology is just like that – a really bad master but a great servant.

You only have to look at people with their mobile phones. Most people carry them around as though they were hard-wired into the tendons in their hands. They're constantly looking at them rather than where they are going. You see them in restaurants and in other public places not talking to one another but texting, each other probably. The amount of time the human race spends in front of screens of one sort or another is astonishing. I mean look at you lot here today, you've all got your mobile phones on the table and keep looking at them and I wonder if you listened to what we've said….."

"Oh, we've heard you alright," said Peter Piper a bit disgruntled.

Gertie went on, "Of course whilst people are so busy with mobile phones they miss the really important things. Not just the wonders of the world, nature, birds singing that sort of thing. Just being in the now. They miss out on all the natural joys and wonders of the world as well as not understanding, not really understanding that is, what's happening right in front of their noses."

All the visitors began shuffling about as listening to Gertie was making them feel very uncomfortable.

She went on, "It's great having the labour-saving devices and the computers and automation but the internet has ruined the shopping on the High Streets – I mean that used to be one of life's simple pleasures – gone! I loved shopping for new outfits and such like. Getting out of the house and meeting people and catching up with all the gossip that sort of thing it all makes you happy. It doesn't really take much and it's not about having a lot of money. Enough for your needs and you're content. Too much money and you start to worry about it and if someone's going to come along and take it all away from you and that leads to stress.

And did you know that the number one killer is stress? Whatever the medical profession may say. Stress causes all sorts of illnesses and brings on some which may never have come about and the problem is that stress is a growth industry as more and more people suffer from it. There's more stress about today than ever before. Just driving in a car can be very stressful, just walking down the street sometimes, going to work or being at home can be equally stressful to some people.

These days the devices people have means that they can be working constantly. They never switch off in some cases. Then there's the social media which is actually a misnomer – its not social media it's anti-social media. People say some terrible things. Why do they do it? I don't know, but there are clearly a lot of unhappy people in this world. The best thing they can do is switch off everything once in a while and just go for a walk. Just live for now, none of this juggling technology, work and home. Just be and just be happy like we are in this Home here.

Now I'm not sure if I've really answered your questions and I'm sorry if I've got on my hobby horse a bit but we live in probably the best of all times. We don't have to go out every day to hunt for food or water. The shops, even the online ones, are full of everything we could possibly need. We live in a country full of abundance and yet people still moan and complain – let them try and go and live in a small African village for a few months and see then what they've got to complain about!

And just one last thing – some people are only happy being unhappy. You know the sort, moaning Minnie's I call them – the glass isn't only half empty but it's bone dry!"

Gertie concluded by saying, "Well there you have it – so ends the sermon!"

Everyone was stunned. Ajay, Brenda and Betty had never heard Gertie be so eloquent and the views she articulated mirrored the values of the Manor Home and Ajay pointed this out.

FB just hummed and ahhed a bit and said, "well that's all as maybe, but don't think you've got away with it. We'll be keeping a very close eye on you lot from now on particularly your applications for grants!"

Cecil had been ineffectually trying to get a word in during Gertie's monologue and finally managed to say, "this is all well and good but it doesn't really answer the questions we need answering and I think we need to have a closer look at this Outing you're planning!"

CHAPTER 8

Betty the Book-Keeper – a Constant Source of Money

The visitors were not happy with the responses the inmates had given and were desperate to score points somehow against the Manor. They said that they now needed to concentrate on the Outing and the costs associated with it and how it all was to be paid for. So it was that Ajay said, "over to you again Betty, perhaps you can explain a bit more about how we account for all of our income and expenditure, you know a bit of history sort of thing, and then run though the figures for the Outing."

Betty had been with the Manor Home for about as long as anyone could remember. When the Care Home Company, CHC, took over the Home, Betty had come along with it almost as part of the fixtures and fittings.

Betty was well past retirement age although she didn't look it and she certainly didn't act it. She was a small lady but still quite slim and would have been regarded as being very attractive just a few years ago. She had a mischievous twinkle in her eye and most people couldn't tell when she was joking or being serious because she always seemed to be smiling. This threw any visitors or auditors off the scent and she was able to get away with the most outrageous assertions.

Now a widow all she really had was her work at the Home and this helped her get through the bad times. She always dressed well and seemed well looked after from a financial perspective. She had a tendency to quote Woody Allen when reimbursing expenses and would say "I've been rich and I've been poor but I prefer rich if only for financial reasons."

Betty prepared the books of account for Henry the accountant to produce the final accounts for the Home each year. Henry had asked Betty to use a computerised system of book-keeping for quite a while now but Betty would always reply that she did not like those 'new-fangled thingies' and anyway it was easy to see where the money was coming and going in her ledger which was the size of a small table and about a foot thick. In fact it almost took three people to carry it and so it always tended to reside on Betty's desk which was in the office area just outside of Ajay's office. It was now in front of the visitors who were still puzzling over it.

In the office area, Betty occupied, there were a couple of 'hot desks' for use by Henry when he was there and also Leeroy to help with his storeroom activities and his new investment administration. In fact the desks were used by several of the staff for personal phone calls and any administrative tasks they need to carry out. Also these desks had desktop computers on them and so staff and residents could do a bit of internet surfing if they wanted to. Both the staff and those residents who were, shall we say, 'switched on' used the computers for updating their Facebook profiles and so on. Burnt Offering and Harry the handyman both used the computers, ostensibly for ordering supplies but also for carrying out research into horse racing, online gambling and for any competitions and such like that took their fancy.

Although there was a constant stream of people coming and going through this general office area, Betty argued that 'The Ledger' was perfectly safe on her desk because it was too heavy to carry off. Also, Betty thought that no one would be able to decipher her particular method of double entry book-keeping which was basically a form of double, double-entry with everything entered in at least four different places within the ledger. Betty reasoned that it was better to record things several times rather than not at all which was commendable but which made any form of reconciliation almost impossible.

Betty had a view that God helps them that help themselves and on those occasions when there just seemed to be no way of balancing the books without some form of adjustment she would simply take out what was needed to restore balance once more. This 'surplus' usually found its way into the pockets of the staff to act as a float for them when they went anywhere with the inmates. This was mainly in respect of outings and there was rarely any change. In fact the staff usually ended up claiming additional expenses mainly due to excessive drinking!

Henry's job, of course, was to audit the transactions as well as producing a final set of accounts and he had initially engaged Betty in discussing the anomalies that he continually kept finding. He had eventually given up as Betty relayed her marathon number of entries and also seemed to engage in bartering and swopping any surplus stores with different suppliers usually using Gertie's grandson Terry and also Peggy's granddaughter Debbie who was able to source medical supplies for the inmates and sometimes for Nurse Brown and for Matron.

Henry referred to Betty's book-keeping as the 'Mickey Mouse school of book-keeping' and had basically given up ever trying to understand it. Whenever he asked Betty for additional information it only confused matters more and so he now tends to accept the figures and marvels at the ever increasing bank balance. Betty proudly informed the visitors, "our accountant, Henry, always signs off my figures, first time, whenever the annual reports need to be completed."

The last time Henry had asked for a simple explanation from Betty she said, "now what you need to understand, dear, is that this is a 'progressive' system whereby we should all end up with more money coming in than going out."

Henry replied that he thought this was simple enough explanation and that basically accountants are simple people who could only deal with two things – money coming in and money going out.

"Exactly!" Betty had said as she went onto explain, "if we get the supplies from Terry or Debbie then they go into a separate column and sometimes the bills from the butcher for Burnt Offering, I mean Tony, go there as well. It's a question of economics see?" to which Henry shook his head. Betty continued, "you're thinking too narrow about arithmetic when I'm talking about statistics see?"

As Henry began to look more and more lost, Betty carried on, "if we have to use real money then that goes here in this column and then when we settle up. I just 'nett off' what I can with whoever I can depending on what they've had from us and what we've had from them. The bartering can become a bit complicated as the value of Terry's stuff might not be the same as what we're trading it for and so it's a sort of 'swings and roundabouts' situation. In fact it's all a bit of a 'broad brush' approach but it seems to work, don't you agree?"

Henry was still shaking his head and was completely lost at this stage and said, "what they've had from you? I don't understand what they can have from you! The Home provides a service in looking after older people, how can there be anything that people have from you?"

"There you go dear, not looking at the bigger picture. You might say I offset one thing against another," said Betty smiling as she continued, "you know a surplus here is offset against a deficit there – I just nett them off and it keeps everything nice and tidy."

Henry just continued to look lost and said, "I still don't see what is actually happening!"

"Well it's all there in black and white dearie," said Betty as she went on, "now do you see why I wouldn't want to use a computer for this? It can get a little confusing unless you can see it all set up like it is in the ledger. The big picture as I call it"

Henry had conceded that the ledger Betty referred to was indeed big enough to contain the big picture but he couldn't see it, not even a little bit of the big picture. He shook his head some more. He was sure he had a migraine coming on and he didn't even have migraines. He concluded that the accounts for the Manor were an even bigger fiction than even he had thought. He said to Betty, "I think I'm beginning to get it Betty. I think we'll just carry on as usual for now eh?"

"Quite right dear," we wouldn't want to over complicate things now would we? Not just when we've got it all working so smoothly," she said with a straight face.

Henry nodded and made his excuses and thought I'll just add a few percentage points to last year's figures and 'back into' the bank account so to speak and no one will know the difference – hopefully.

Following this somewhat lengthy and anecdotal explanation of how the system worked FB was shaking her head and said, "do you understand any of this Cecil? It looks like it's deliberately designed to confuse!"

Cecil Humphries was the 'numbers man' as they called him. His training was in the actuarial field for pension funds but he'd found that too exiting and moved into mainstream accounting which he thought suited him better as it was far more sedate.

He said, "well it's got its merits I suppose. It is a very comprehensive record even if it is a bit difficult to follow."

"But is the money being spent wisely?" asked Sadiq.

"I think so," said Cecil much to FB's annoyance. He went on, "the activities and especially the Outing are well attended and there's no doubt the residents get a lot out of this sort of thing and so I feel I must conclude that, after due deliberation," he waffled, "that this particular home is very well run."

FB couldn't believe her ears. She turned to Peter Piper only to see him nodding his agreement.

"Well, that all seems to be satisfactory then after all," said Ajay, "thank you Betty. Now has anyone anything else they would like to add?"

FB was clearly not happy and looked around the table trying to find an excuse to block future grants. She said, "OK that's all for now but I repeat that we shall be watching you and your grant applications very carefully from now on."

All of the Social Services seemed happy enough although Stella still thought the inmates needed some form of indoctrination into the 'real world'. Also, none of the Local Authority visitors seemed to be supporting FB and so she asked Leonard if there was anything further he needed. Leonard shook his head and Ajay asked, "now would you all like to join us for lunch?"

FB was about to shake her head when she noted that all of the other visitors were nodding. After the excellent chocolate biscuits they had consumed they thought that an even more excellent lunch would finish the morning off nicely.

And so it was that the Manor Care Home continued along in its own inimitable way. The rest of the week passed relatively quickly with all the coming and goings, wheeling and dealing, buying and selling and all financed by a fair amount of creativity by Henry and Ajay firmly based on Betty's book-keeping.

Betty had provided floats for the staff members going on the Outing and asked for receipts as always but she knew it very unlikely that any would be forthcoming. She thought that she should go on one of these outings one of the years to see what they all get up to.

CHAPTER 9

Thursday Evening – the eve of the Outing

On the Thursday evening Ajay and Matron had discussed providing medication or booze or both to the inmates to help them sleep. Matron thought that sleeping pills might mean that the residents would not wake up in time for the coach and so a few bottles of beer, whisky and gin had miraculously appeared courtesy of Betty's system of floats. The staff said it was what was left over from the previous Christmas but the residents knew better as Terry had arrived with a white van laden down with something heavy.

After Terry had finished in the office he popped round to the communal living room and had a chat with Gertie. The Manor's living rooms or communal areas consisted of a large living room which had been the central room for entertaining when the house was first built and had been extensively extended and decorated since then. The carpet could be rolled back which revealed a dance floor which was used for certain social occasions and also for keep fit classes. The residents at the Manor were very fortunate that they were encouraged to partake of as many activities as possible. All the staff, led by the Matron, were constantly reminded of the need to keep the residents active. This not only kept them fit but also kept at bay the ever-increasing threat of dementia and other diseases. It also avoided the need for 'just sleeping' signs around the inmates necks which were there to stop the staff calling the undertakers.

The other communal areas consisted of the library, a games

room and a TV lounge but again residents were not allowed just to sit and watch television for hours on end. Any programme that provided mental stimulus and particularly activity programmes based around hobbies and the like were greatly encouraged and all of the residents at the Manor were far more active and fit and healthy as a result of this policy.

The games room was nearly always occupied by a set of four playing bridge as well as a couple of chess players or other card players at different tables set out for those games. All sorts of board games were available. Similarly the library was extensively used for looking up facts and figures, or carrying out a bit of research, to support the debates that tend to stem out of 'rose tinted' thinking rather than actual facts. This was supported by the internet surfing which took place in the office area near Betty. It was all done very amicably and the residents thrived on keeping their mental faculties generally in full working order.

Gertie was sitting in her usual chair in the communal living room and said' "you all set for tomorrow, Terry? Going to be an early start you know?"

Terry replied, "don't you worry about me Nan, I'm all ready to go and I'll be here in time before the coach leaves."

Gertie looked around to make sure that no one was listening and said, "have you managed to sort out that bit of transportation to take us to the racecourse?"

Terry also gave a furtive look around and said, "it's all taken care of Nan. I've had a word with Harry and he reckons providing we match the carers and relatives to the trip within a trip we'll be OK."

Gertie thought for a moment and said, "well there'll be you and me, the General and Bert who Harry'll look after. Then there's Peggy and Eric and of course Burnt Offering will be coming – he wouldn't miss a day at the races. So that's eight of us for Redcar!"

"Shh…" said Terry looking round, "not so loud, we don't want

Matron or any others of the staff getting wind of this or they'll all want to come and the people carrier that me and Harry have sorted out won't take them all."

"Mum's the word," said Gertie placing a finger to her lips just like how a child would.

Terry shook his head and said, "don't you get drinking too much of that gin that I've bought in tonight. You need to be 'bright eyed and bushy tailed' for tomorrow if we're going to take those bookies to the cleaners."

With that Terry got up to leave and Harry escorted him to the door to confirm all their arrangements as they went.

Meanwhile another breakaway faction was forming under the leadership of Beryl and Elizabeth with Old Joe egging them on. They were the only ones in the TV room and pretending to watch a documentary about saving the planet from cows farting.

Beryl was saying, "I don't think I could be a vegetarian, I like a proper dinner me, you know, meat and two veg."

"Will you concentrate on what Elizabeth is saying and come away from that telly?" said Old Joe.

Elizabeth had got it into her head that Robin Hood was not only real but lived quite close to Whitby in Robin Hood's Bay. Beryl and Old Joe had tried to convince her that this was not the case but Elizabeth was having none of it.

Elizabeth had found out that Robin Hood's Bay was only a few miles from Whitby by using the computers in the main office area. She assured the others that she had been very discrete and was in the process of convincing them that they could take a taxi from Whitby to the Robin Hood's Bay and be back in time for the fish and chip supper before anyone knew they were gone.

Old Joe kept saying, "I don't know, you know, about taxis and that."

To which Elizabeth replied, "well I do, you know. We'll be sharing the cost if that's what you're worrying about?"

Beryl thought the reason Old Joe kept going on about taxis was because he could be a bit on the 'tight' side when it came to paying for anything.

Old Joe was shaking his head rather vigorously when Elizabeth said, "look, I'll pay for the taxi if you're worried about it. All you have to do is to be able to flag one down and get us in there before anyone knows we've gone."

Old Joe visibly relaxed when he realised that he wouldn't need to pay for the taxi and he became quite enthusiastic once more, "no problem, I can flag down a taxi at fifty paces, no problem."

Beryl reminded them, "there's going to be eight of us all together. Us three and Elizabeth's granddaughter Rebecca, Cyril and Mary. Elizabeth has also had a chat with Priya and Mo to come along as our carers for the trip."

There were now no takers for the visit to Dracula's grave. The potential grave visitors had frightened themselves with outlandish stories and superstitions and therefore now intended to remain with the other inmates going on the Outing who had settled for a day at the seaside.

Both of the sub-groups, for the races and Robin Hood's Bay, plotted their trips within trips and all that could be heard throughout the communal areas was fevered whisperings which, because of the hard of hearing of some of the inmates, snippets could be overheard such as "well he won at Ripon the other day" and "Oh yes, he definitely moved up to Whitby from Nottingham" and "well so long as we're back for the fish and chip supper."

The drinks were served on that Thursday evening by the carers who were also very excited about the trip the next day.

Eric said to Mo, "it'll make a change for us all to be out and about.

I just need to let you know that me and Harry will be taking a small group out from the main group to the races at Redcar. Not a word now to anybody and especially don't say anything to Matron or Ajay."

"Funny you should mention that Eric, because me and Priya plan to go a short way up the coast with a few of the inmates to Robin Hood's Bay," said Mo.

Eric looked at her and said, "have you cleared it with anybody?

"No," said Mo, "but we'll be back well in time for the fish and chips and I don't think there's much there anyway. It's just that Elizabeth's got this bee in her bonnet about Robin Hood actually existing and that he lived in Robin Hood's Bay or some such thing like that."

Eric said, "well if you keep my secret then I'll keep yours."

"Deal," said Mo, "should be a good day out for us all. But what about Matron, Eric. I can't even think of a word to describe how she'll react if she finds out that half the group have gone off on their own personalised 'jollies'. You know what she's like! She could make a sergeant major blush once she gets started. I mean she'll have a temper of monumental proportions once she finds out."

"Well, we'll make sure that she's got enough going on to keep her busy," said Eric mysteriously.

And so the plans were hatched that evening in various parts of the Home. Each of the different groups didn't want the others knowing what they intended to do and, as they all started to wonder off to bed after their drinks, they were all displaying knowing smiles whilst wishing their 'good nights' to each other. The staff were thinking watch out Whitby you don't know what's going to hit you tomorrow. Possibly the biggest bunch of rogues and renegades that you have ever seen!

CHAPTER 10

The big day arrives

On the day of the Outing it started pretty much the same as the usual chaos that existed every other day. The fact that today was going to be a day out for the staff and the inmates hadn't fully registered yet. People were still waking up and although the inmates had been reminded about six or seven times it only gradually permeated the old grey matter so that everyone began mumbling 'day out' and 'seaside' and such like. A lot of this, of course, was to do with the consumption of copious amounts of alcohol the previous evening.

"It's an absolute bloody chaos out there!" shouted Matron, "the inmates are all lining up to get on the coach and they haven't even had their breakfast or medication yet!"

The General who'd already started on his hip flask said, "Matron, it's simple entropy, you know?"

"What on Earth are you going on about now General?" Matron replied.

"It's the second law of thermodynamics, which states that things have a natural tendency towards disorder, as in it is easier to mess things up and in so many ways, but there is only one way to do things tidily." Said the General who then sauntered off to refill his hip flask leaving Matron even more bewildered than before.

Ajay, who was dreading this outing for all sorts of reasons, looked at everyone milling around in the main reception area or in the communal living room and said, "they're just a little bit over excited, that's all." Matron was right though it was chaotic. Carers and staff were just as excited as the inmates and there was much toing and froing and the flapping of arms. Ajay thought it best to stay out of the way and see if he could come up with a credible excuse not to go on the trip again this year and so he retired to his office to look through some paperwork to see if he could drum up a meeting with someone. He had no intention of going even though it was expected of him. Each year he'd manage to come up with a plausible excuse to duck out at the last minute and this year would be no exception.

Matron was getting more and more agitated and her face had taken on a sort of red like hue which didn't bode well for anyone who got in her way. She was shouting at Nurse Brown and Eric to get the breakfast and medication sorted. Unfortunately it was a case of 'more haste, less speed' as 'sod's law' dictated that whatever could go wrong did, in fact go wrong and on multiple occasions. Eric and Nurse Brown were wrestling with getting those inmates to have their breakfast before their medication and those that took their medication after food.

The Nurse had roped in Mo and Sharon to help with the dispensing of the medication. Eric, Leeroy and Priya were rounding up the inmates to get them into the dining room to have their breakfasts. Inevitably mistakes were going to be made especially as Sharon found it difficult to retain any instructions for longer than a millisecond. So it was that she found herself with pink and green tablets and facing Gertie and Peggy and began a somewhat convoluted thought process, "now was it pink for Gertie and green for Peggy" she was saying to herself.

"What, what's that, you said," shouted Gertie, who like some of the others, was partially deaf but thought that it was people that mumbled rather than her hearing and she would complain rather loudly that people should really speak up.

Sharon said, "I was trying to remember who has which tablets. Gertie, do you have these pink ones?"

"No not me Dear, what are they like? Are they any good?" replied Gertie.

Just then Peggy butted in and said, "no, I think I'm on pink, but I could be wrong. These days I take so many tablets it's a wonder I don't rattle."

Sharon became more confused as she "ummed and ahhed…" without coming to any conclusion.

"I know," said Peggy, "let's ask Jim."

Gertie and Sharon didn't know who Peggy meant and so both of them looked at the tablets and then at each other before Gertie realised and said, "you mean Eric you silly so and so."

"That's right Jim… Eric… whatever," said Peggy who was sometimes 'away with the fairies' before she'd even taken her tablets.

Sharon was losing it big time at this stage and thought she might as well take the tablets herself and have done with it.

Gertie said, "I think the best thing is if we have one of each. That way each of us will have at least half of what we should have."

Sharon couldn't fault this logic and so handed out one pink tablet and one green tablet each to Gertie and Peggy.

They were both about to take them when Matron shouted, "STOP!" at the top of her voice. All of the inmates and the staff stopped what they were doing – there was a general clattering of cutlery and some of the inmates were in the middle of taking medication and couldn't decide whether to swallow or not. Others were on their way to the dining room and some were just wandering around in an aimless fashion. But everything, literally everything, came to a halt.

The Matron, who now had everyone's attention, most with a fearful look in their eyes, said, a bit more calmly, "do not take any medication, give whatever you've got back to Nurse Brown. Go into the dining room and finish your breakfast if you've started it and Nurse Brown and I will come around to you to dispense the medication."

No one moved. Staff and inmates just looked at one another until Matron shouted, "Now, go into the dining room Now!"

Peggy and Gertie were slightly disappointed about not being able to have one of each of the pink and green tablets and thought Matron to be a bit of a spoilsport. As people started to shuffle towards the dining room Matron said, "not you Sharon and Maureen, you need to come with me and explain exactly who's had what medication."

So a potential medical catastrophe was avoided and the inmates eventually received the correct tablets, more or less, albeit that one or two of the inmates would have an interesting day because of the additional incorrect tablets that some had already taken. There was definitely a glint in the General's eye but this could have had something to do with his hip flask that he thought he should 'test out' earlier and having topped it up again, "need to make sure it's working properly" he was overheard to say.

Because most of the residents at the Manor were well into their eighties many of them suffered with memory lapses and all of them were on medication for one ailment or another. Sometimes this was a fairly benign type ailment such as diarrhoea or constipation. In many cases it was high blood pressure or high cholesterol levels. The inmates were well looked after at the Manor and this together with their extracurricular activities meant that on the whole they were a pretty robust bunch in spite of their advancing years.

The noise in the dining room was deafening and Matron again had to shout to inform the inmates that she and Nurse Brown would be coming round to each table with the correct medication for each person. Matron tried to get the inmates to understand that if they had already had their medication then they needed to tell the nurse or her so as not to repeat the dosage. As most of the inmates couldn't remember where they had been five minutes ago, let alone what they had been doing this was a bit of a 'tall order'.

Due to the excitement, noise, incorrect and too much medication a combination of factors meant that they left the Manor a lot later than planned. Messy eating and frequent trips to the toilet were the two main reasons why nearly all the staff and inmates had to change their outfits and some on more than one occasion.

"Isn't it exciting?" said Gertie to Elizabeth as they waited for Gertie's grandson, Terry and Elizabeth's granddaughter, Rebecca to arrive.

"I'm really looking forward to it," replied Elizabeth.

Gertie looked around her and said as quietly as she could manage, "if you don't see much of us at Whitby, don't worry, but there's a small group of us off to the races at Redcar."

Elizabeth smiled and said, "really? Well you're not the only ones who plan to have some time away from Whitby."

Gertie looked a bit puzzled and Elizabeth went on, "yes, there's a small group that I'm going to go with to have a look for Robin Hood."

"Do you mean Robin Hood's Bay?" asked Gertie.

"Well yes, that's where he'll be, of course, Robin Hood will be in Robin Hood's Bay!"

Elizabeth smiled and continued, "you won't say anything will you?"

Gertie said, "I won't be there to say anything. Anyway we need to be discrete about the races as well."

"OK, well perhaps we'll catch up later at Whitby," said Elizabeth and with that they both went off to change again and to go to the toilet – again.

Ajay came running out of his office and shouted to his assistant, Brenda, that he wouldn't after all be able to go on the trip now and that she would need to go and deputise for him. Since Brenda had planned to go anyway this was no problem but she thought that she would find out what Ajay's excuse was this year and said, "what's the problem Ajay, why is it that you won't be able to come?"

Ajay looked to be deep in thought for a moment when he suddenly snapped his fingers and said, "that's it, I mean, er.... that ....I shall have to stay behind because, because, well because the meter reader is coming and I want to make sure that we get charged correctly for the gas and electricity we use!"

"Really," said Brenda, "couldn't Betty do that? After all she'll be the one who pays the bill."

Ajay looked like he'd been caught with is hand in the cookie jar as he said, "Oh no, I couldn't ask Betty to do that. No, not with all the work she's got on at the moment. It just wouldn't be fair now, would it?"

Brenda said, "I thought Betty usually looked after that side of things," not letting him off the hook too readily.

"No, it's got to me," said Ajay with some determination, "you'll have a nice time and Betty'll let you have a float to buy a drink for everyone on the way back."

"OK then," said Brenda, "I'll do that" and Ajay just smiled and hurried off back to his office out of harm's way.

Matron and Nurse Brown had finally managed to confirm that everyone had had at least some of their medication if not twice the amount that they should have had. Most of the inmates had also managed to eat some breakfast in between excited chatter and frequent trips to the toilets. Brenda said to Matron and Nurse Brown, "I shall be deputising for Ajay, yet again, but as far as I'm concerned you'll be running the show Matron. Just let me know if you want me to do anything. I'll just tag along and you won't know I'm there."

The inmates were led out of the Home a little bit like children in a 'crocodile' formation and holding onto one another for dear life. Eric, Mo and Priya were shepherding them towards the coach but each time one got on it seemed like two got off.

Burnt Offering and Harry decided to lend a hand and they started to get more on the coach than there were waiting in the car park.

"We're winning," Harry was saying just before Elizabeth and Mary came down the steps of the coach saying that they needed to find Elizabeth's granddaughter, Rebecca.

Then it was Gertie's turn looking for her grandson, Terry, and then the General and Bert needed the toilet yet again.

Eventually the coach filled up and the carers, Matron and the Nurse looked around the car park for any 'strays' and couldn't really believe that they had actually managed to get them all on and ready to go.

Eric said, "quick let's get on and get away otherwise we'll be here all day!"

The coach driver and tour guide looked like they couldn't believe it after what they'd been through that morning.

CHAPTER 11

All aboard - The coach is waiting

The coach had arrived at the time booked which was an incredibly optimistic time of 7:00 am. Who quite thought that time up needed their head looking at. It was clearly evident from previous trips that they would not be able to get a couple of dozen elderly people ready by that time.

It was a big coach which could accommodate some forty people quite easily. The total number going on the outing was thirty something or other at the last count. Not that counting was much of an issue. When the coach looked reasonably full it would just get going and anyone left behind would have to make their own way.

The coach now had on board the inmates and those of their relatives that had foolishly agreed to accompany them. Also there were the staff from the Manor Home who would be going with them on the outing. The final number therefore which actually made it onto the coach could be anywhere between thirty and forty.

Gertie's grandson Terry had arrived together with Elizabeth's granddaughter, Rebecca. Both hoped to conduct a bit of business before they set out.

There had been a mid-week supplies crisis of sorts and Terry had arrived not only with his paper products but also with other supplies mainly in the nature of toiletries, make-up and underwear. Terry proceeded to unload these on Leeroy who was desperately trying to find somewhere to store them. Terry and Leeroy would each take a cut of the sale proceeds of these items and Leeroy had told Terry that he could help him shift more of his product if he included him on the deals.

Elizabeth meanwhile was busy on her granddaughter's mobile phone to her broker placing buy and sell orders in accordance with Rebecca's latest instructions. Rebecca's share tips would appear in the week-end papers and so it was important to get the transactions booked now so that when Monday rolled around the buy/sell orders could be reversed and, as Elizabeth called it, "a pleasant little profit" could be shared between Rebecca and her when the time was right. The money would be held in each of the nominee accounts, they used for this purpose, which made it difficult for anybody to track down the transactions later on.

When the coach had arrived at the home it had managed to reverse onto the car park so that the inmates could embark more easily. This didn't really make much difference to the chaotic embarkation than ensued but the driver thought it was a 'nice touch'. The driver, however, looked to be older than some of the inmates who were going on the trip. Driving had been in his family for years. His Dad, who had died in his sleep after failing to hear the screams from his passengers, as he plunged over a steep cliff, had passed on many tips for successful driving journeys before that fateful day.

The driver was called Derick and, in spite of requests that people should use his full name, he was invariably referred to as Del. Sometimes this was turned into 'Del the Driver'. This was usually before he'd taken people out on the coach as the names he was called afterwards ranged from 'Dangerous Derick' to 'Death Wish Del'. These were the polite versions most of the obscenities were shouted at him to try to keep him on the road and the coach in one piece. He was incredibly superstitious and was an avid reader of his horoscope each day. Consequently he always seemed to have an air of foreboding about him.

Gertie thought he was wonderful though, and had took to him immediately, because she thought she had 'the gift' of divination, fortune telling and other esoteric activities. Once she and Del got talking there was no stopping them and the outcome of the trip would hang in the balance for the rest of the day. Whatever took place, Gertie and Derick would claim that they foresaw it happening and mumble to themselves about people not being tuned into the spirits. To which replies invariably went along the lines "spirits, spirits? He's got half a bottle of Johnnie Walker in him already. He don't need any more spirits!"

The tour guide, who also came with the coach, was a smooth young fascist who thought that euthanasia was a good thing and if he had his way this lot would be the first to go. He was arrogant, self-centred and had a Narcissistic complex which in his case was probably the real thing rather than just an infatuation. About thirty years old, of medium height and weight but with a hairstyle that had a life of its own. His real name was Wayne but he liked to be known as 'Clint'. Some of the older men would miss out the 'n' from his name much to his annoyance but the inmates thought that it was very appropriate and that it described him and his manner and nature to a 'T'.

Wayne/Clint was hoping from foot to foot in frustration at trying to get everyone on board. Cyril said to him, "if you need to go to the toilet I'd go now if I were you. That tour guide looks a bit of a one."

"I am the tour guide you idiot!" shouted Wayne.

"Are you?" replied Cyril, "well you're not making a very good job of it are you?"

To which Wayne just walked off shaking his and shouting at anyone in his line of fire. "will you please just get on the f…, ff….-flipping coach" he kept saying.

The inmates had eventually started to line up on the car park again in two's, often holding hands like kindergarten children do. The 'crocodile' line moved very slowly mainly because everyone started to check that they had got everything. Each time, when someone on the staff asked one of them if they'd got their glasses/pills/cardigan/coat/ comfortable shoes/other medications and so on then everyone would have to check. Every time someone mentioned one of the items the whole line would check all over again and again.

The line meandered across the car park without actually ever seeming to embark anyone onto the coach. Derick was getting more and more agitated as Gertie kept saying, "see I told you so, didn't I? When the moons in a conjunction like this it always brings disorder and chaos."

Derick looked on dolefully and wondered if they would ever get the passengers on and get away. They were already well over an hour later than they had planned for the departure and a further contingent had just got off the coach to go to the toilet once more. This was in spite of Derick letting them all know that there was a toilet on board. After which he'd overheard one of the ladies talking to her friend saying, "I can't go when the things moving, can you? I mean it's not natural going when it's going at thirty miles an hour. It's no good I shall have to go again now before we go!"

Derick was becoming more and more anxious. He'd consulted his horoscope, conversed with Gertie who'd also read his tea leaves and he had his lucky rabbits foot. But he kept thinking to himself about what could go wrong this time. It seemed ages since he'd had an event free trip. The delay in setting off didn't bode well at all and by the time they got to Whitby there would be a great deal of traffic about. Derick didn't deal with traffic very well. He could never seem to keep up with the flow and quite frequently suffered torrents of abuse from frustrated car drivers waiting to overtake.

Derek was recalling previous day trips where unfortunately disaster had struck. It wasn't his fault really and anyway he had got lot thicker glasses now. In fact his glasses were so think he could almost see into the future with them now. That crane that they'd used to haul the coach out of the drainage ditch, the other day, did the trick OK, he thought, and he hoped they could get hold of that again should the need arise.

He decided to have a chat to Gertie to try and assuage his anxiety. "its not looking good Gertie. We should have been away a good hour ago. My stars said an early start was most auspicious but that later in the day there was an adverse conjunction that'll do me no good whatsoever."

"Don't worry dear," said Gertie, "I'm here and I can't see anything to interfere with having a good day out."

"You're not driving though are you?" Said Derick.

"No, but I can help you navigate can't I?" said Gertie.

Derick looked relived and said, "would you Gertie? That would be a tremendous help to me. You know the tour guide, Wayne, Clint whatever he calls himself, well he gets a bit annoyed with me especially when I don't know where I'm going. I've got this Sat Nav that's got a mind of it's own. It seems as though it's always telling me off for going the wrong way. It's a woman's voice, in the Sat Nav but she sounds so severe as though she's constantly annoyed about something. It's most upsetting"

Gertie was about to say something else but Derick was off on one his laments, "not only does he get mad with me, Wayne that is, but when I don't know where I'm going he also shouts at me when I take those corners on two sets of wheels instead of four. I mean I don't always see things until I'm right on top of them even with these new glasses. He doesn't like it when I stop – too sudden he says, he doesn't like it when I start – not smooth enough he tells me. I tell you my nerves and ready to go on holiday. All the shouting and sniping, I might as well stay at home and let the wife tell me off instead."

"Oh dear," said Gertie, "someone's got themselves into a bit of state haven't they?"

"I've only had the one drink Gertie, honest," replied Derick

"No silly, I mean letting that Wayne character get to you like that. I'll be sitting right behind you and if he goes off on one I'll give him what for, you mark my words!" said Gertie with some determination.

This seemed to placate Derick and he and Wayne once again walked up and down the coach to try and get some idea if they were ready to go.

There were the grown-up children and/or grandchildren along with inmates which together with the staff meant the coach looked pretty full. As this was considered 'close enough', Eric shouted for Del the Driver to get going. Eric was sitting at the front and was saying to the driver, "you've got a lot of time to catch up driver."

Derick just rolled his eyes which was not a pretty sight behind the 'pebble bottoms' that passed as glasses for him. He made the sign of the cross and looked at Gertie as he engaged first gear.

Gertie and Terry were just behind Derick on the other side of the coach and Gertie kept saying that everything was going to be fine. It would have instilled a bit more confidence in the passengers if Derick didn't keep looking round at her instead of concentrating on the road. He was continually touching what would have been his forelock if he had any hair left and Terry said to him, "that's a nasty twitch you've got there driver."

Derick said, "it's not a twitch, I'm saluting the magpies. You know, the birds, 'one for sorrow, two for joy….. well when you see only one you can avoid the sorrow by saluting it."

"How does it know? asked Terry.

"Well if you're going to scoff and scorn, I sharn't discuss it with you any further," and with that Derick turned around to see where he was going which was a good thing as he was just in time to narrowly avoid shunting the rear end of a rather large SUV.

CHAPTER 12

Whitby here we come – 'It's better to travel in hope than arrive'

Wayne, or Clint as he preferred to be called, was sitting next to Eric in the front seats level with the driver, when Derick had come out with this quote saying that it's better to travel in hope than arrive.

"What sort of a saying's that?" said Eric as Wayne just rolled his eyes and whispered to Eric, "don't encourage him, he'll be away telling you all sorts of rubbish once he gets started on this sort of thing."

Derick looked a bit non-plussed and said, "I don't really know, but it's a well-known saying that is! Well almost, I think, I might have got the words slightly wrong, and I think it's more to do with trains than coaches but the sentiments there isn't it?"

Elizabeth, who although was a little way back, managed to overhear the conversation between Eric and Derick and shouted forward to them that it was actually "To travel hopefully is a better thing than to arrive."

Both Eric and Derick turned to look back at her much to the alarm of Gertie and Terry in the other front seats who shouted out "will you keep your eyes on the road!"

Elizabeth continued that it was Robert Louis Stevenson who had originally made this quote meaning that hope and anticipation are often better than the ultimate reality.

Terry said, "well that's certainly true of our current reality.

We've got a coach full of geriatrics being driven by a short-sighted, nervous wreck who salutes magpies for heaven's sake."

"Now Terry, don't you mock what you don't understand, there's a good boy," said Gertie slightly disapproving of Terry's cavalier approach to the mystical workings of the universe. "Derick knows what he's doing and we mustn't tempt fate now must we?"

Terry just shook his head and said, "Nan, it's all a load of baloney!"

Gertie was shaking her head and saying, "oh no it's not Terry, and Derick is in tune with the universe. He doesn't particularly have the gift like me but he's in contact with the spirit world."

Eric piped up, "well a few of us saw him having a nip before we set off and so I suppose he is in touch with some spirits. The question is how much spirits. He doesn't look too sound as it is and if he's been drinking as well…."

Wayne interrupted, "don't worry about that. He actually drives better with a drink inside of him."

Most of the coach had been listening to this exchange – well those that didn't need hearing aids anyway, and they laughed at this until they realised it meant Derick could be driving 'three sheets to the wind' to use an expression that one of them came up with. The laughter turned to a sort of whimper followed by an eerie silence.

Derick of course was oblivious to the rather tense atmosphere behind him and just tootled along a little too fast really for the roads they were on. It was ironic that he would speed up on unsuitable smaller roads and slow down on the main 'A' roads. He started trying to whistle a song. It was a tuneless rendition of a very old song about three wheels on my wagon and I'm still rolling along. Needless to say this did not instil any confidence into his passengers who were gradually becoming more and more nervous.

Gertie had always fancied herself as a bit of a clairvoyant and was saying to Terry that she could come over 'all funny' at the drop of a hat. Terry thought she would come all over funny once she was on the gin but was only half listening as he was watching Derick's driving. He said to Wayne, "are you sure he's passed his test for a coach like this?"

"Oh yes," said Wayne, with his fingers crossed, "he passed a long time ago now."

Terry said, "it was for a motorised coach though wasn't it? Not a coach and a couple of horses."

Wayne just ignored this comment but one or two inmates towards the back heard it and smiled and started singing the song about three wheels on my wagon and I'm still rolling along with some gusto. They reasoned that if they've gotta go they might as well go with a song in their hearts and a smile on their faces.

So the journey continued and everyone made themselves as comfortable as they could which wasn't all that easy when Derick swerved at the last minute around another bend in the road that he didn't seem to notice. He just couldn't seem to match his driving to the prevailing road conditions! Almost standing up, to look through the front windows of the coach, because of his short-sightedness didn't help matters. In spite of his thick glasses Derick's eyesight was not really what it should have been to say the least.

"This reminds me of when we went to Skegness," said Cyril, who was sitting by his granddaughter Becky.

"Why's that?" asked Becky.

"Well the coach, a bit like this one, was roughly split into three different groups and each group decided to see who could outdo the others by having the best time," said Cyril as he went onto explain about the number of pubs the inmates visited. He continued, "the one who went to the most pubs was the winner, but the trouble was no one could remember how many pubs they'd been into and at least one pub was visited on more than one occasion and double counting led to a disqualification anyway!"

Becky said, "well I hope we won't be having any of that behaviour today. I know I'm not on duty but I'm still a WPC and I have standards to uphold!"

"Quite right, love," said Cyril, "but why don't you take a day off today eh? Today you're my granddaughter and you're going to enjoy yourself for once eh?"

"Oh alright Dad," replied Becky, "I suppose I can turn a 'blind eye' for one day."

"That's my girl," said Cyril thankfully.

Just behind Cyril and Becky was Tom Baxter known as Soups Baxter, or just Soups, and sitting next to him was Old Joe. Both Soups and Old Joe kept themselves busy one way or another and were telling 'war stories' about jobs and escapades that they had been involved with in the past. This was a bit risky because Cyril and Becky could overhear them and Soups was saying, "course things are a lot more tricky these days Joe, you can't just knock out something that looks similar very often I need an original document to copy from."

Old Joe said, "Oh the worlds definitely changing Soups and not always for the better. You take my game. I do a bit of consulting now again for businesses and it used to pay really well for not particularly doing much work."

"You know what they say about consultants don't you?" asked Soups.

"Yeah, I've heard them all before; 'a consultant is someone who borrows your watch to tell you the time' and there was another one doing the rounds recently as 'what do you call a consultant at the bottom of the sea?"

Soups just shook his head and Old Joe concluded, "a good start!"

"The one I liked," said Soups laughing, "was the one about consultants keep turning up like a turd that won't flush away," and he laughed aloud.

"Anyway," Old Joe continued, "as I was saying the world of work has changed a great deal and these days an 'ounce of image is worth a pound of performance'. You take that last job I was on. I'm in a meeting with this manager and he's coming out with every cliché and buzz word known to man. What's known as a 'buzz word wally', and so I start to try and match him buzz word for buzz word and we're talking outside the box and pushing the inside of the envelope with a bit of blue sky thinking and of course we have to have a new paradigm to understand all this."

Soups was laughing and Old Joe thought it was the first time he had seen him lighten up. Usually Soups Baxter could be a very serious and sometimes morose person. The trip must be doing him good already he thought.

On another seat were Bert and the General and having worked out their strategy for the races they were now discussing the General's favourite topic – the state of the nation.

The General was saying, "frankly, I do not share in the deluded view that the government should do everything for everybody, which is what I was trying to say to those visitors the other day. Why it's tantamount to the Nanny State. No I don't want any of that thank you very much!"

"But don't you think that there is moral obligation for the government to help those less fortunate?" asked Bert.

"I think Maggie Thatcher had got it right although I would never have told her to her face," the General was saying when Bert interrupted and said, "did you know Maggie Thatcher then?"

The General sort of bluffed and blustered and mumbled, "only on nodding terms you understand," before launching into what could have been described as his election manifesto had he been canvassing for a seat in parliament.

He was saying, "I mean you've got this government coming out with a potent mix of half-truths and total bollocks haven't you? They say that there are so many million people on the poverty line, as an example, then proceed to donate billions to other countries instead of helping the poor in this country. Not that I particularly believe in handouts. I think people should be able to stand on their own two feet. There are plenty of opportunities for people these days and if they take the time to get themselves educated the worlds their oyster."

"Not everyone can succeed though, can they? Asked Bert.

"No, well there's always an element of what's called 'natural selection', you know, survival of the fittest, and all that, but provided everyone can compete on fairly equal terms then at least it's as equitable as it's going to be. There will always be the winners and the losers in all walks of life," said the General warming to his theme of personal responsibility and people having 'a bit of backbone'.

Bert said, "I'm not so sure, I think there is a moral duty for the government to help the less fortunate."

The General gave Bert what he considered to be a stern look and said, "look here Bert, there will always be people who need help for one reason or another, but the vast majority of people should pull themselves up by their bootstraps instead of getting someone else to pay or blaming someone else if it doesn't turn out right. A lot of the young people today want everything on a plate and they want it straightaway. They don't want to work for it and they expect it as their entitlement as well! They see these footballers on obscene amounts of money or so-called celebrities who've never done a day's work in their life and that's what they want - an easy life with all the rewards but without having to work for it!"

Bert just nodded and thought best to get back to the racing

pages or he'd have to suffer these right-wing rantings until they reached Whitby.

"What did you say you fancied in the three thirty?" he said.

Conversations continued up and down the coach as people 'put the world to rights' and inevitably a central theme was that things were not as good today as they were in the past. Comments such as 'nothings as good as it was' and they don't make things to last any more' and 'even nostalgia's not what it used to be' could be heard up and down the coach. Most of the sayings were repeated because the inmates couldn't remember saying them before and if they did they thought they were always worth repeating anyway.

The people on the coach were roughly divided up into the three groups; there were the Redcar race goers, the Robin Hood's Bay adventurers and the rest who thought that Whitby would be more than enough excitement for them.

The race goers had the sporting pages open and were whispering amongst themselves as to which horses were worth backing. Most of them had raided savings, piggy banks or borrowed off others in order to place 'decent sized bets'.

The Robin Hood's Bay group had maps and various stories about the bay and Robin Hood. The others kept looking at what they were up to although no one really believed that they would venture out on their own on such a half-baked idea.

The last group were happy enough as they were. This group tended to consist of the traditionalists and the sound of papers being unwrapped from barley sugar sweets was deafening at one stage although most of them now appeared to be asleep.

Matron was naturally suspicious of all the whisperings going on about trips within this trip and said to Nurse Brown, "we're going to have to watch them closely today. I've a feeling there's more than one sub plot at work from what I've been able to overhear."

Nurse Brown wasn't too sure what Matron meant and said, "well, we have all the carers with us as well as some of the other staff and so I think we'll be alright."

"Famous last words," thought Matron, "famous last words."

Just then Eric appeared by their seats and said, "Matron, Nurse, I've managed to get some free passes to the Victorian Museum at Whitby and also there's an exhibition of landscape photography that I'm sure some of the inmates would like to have a look at."

"That's very kind of you Eric," said Matron taking the tickets and looking at them.

Nurse Brown said, "there doesn't seem enough for everyone Eric?"

"No," said Eric, "it might not suit everybody and anyway I could only get those. Still I expect most of them will want to go on the beach won't they? But I thought it's something to have in reserve in case any of them get fed up," he added wishing that he'd had a bit more time for Soups to forge a few more of the tickets.

CHAPTER 13

Whitby and a Day at the Races

The coach finally arrived at Whitby just before lunch even though it was only usually a one hour trip from the Home. But with the late start and the (several) toilet stops along the way it was just about mid-day when they parked the coach in a long stay coach park. Del the Driver had managed at the third attempt to get the coach lined up and facing in the right direction for when they departed later on.

Disembarkation was almost as much of a hassle as when they set out which seemed a lifetime ago now. Gertie, Terry and the General started rounding up the Redcar group in a discrete way.

As it was lunch time, the picnic of sandwiches and cakes that had been put on board, needed to be distributed and the carers Eric, Mo and Priya were busy getting it out of the luggage compartment. Derick and Wayne just stood and watched until Eric said, "don't exert yourselves, will you?" To which Wayne said, "come on Del, give them a hand, I don't want to be hanging round this car park all day, I've got places to go."

Del said, "I need to calm down a bit first Wa... Clint... like, you know, ... I'm knackered from all that driving!"

Wayne replied, "well I can't do it can I? I don't want to muck up me clothes, do I? I mean I'll be out on the pull this afternoon and some lucky girl will want me looking nice won't they?"

Del rolled his eyes thinking, "I pity the poor sod that ends up with him" and mumbled something about him being a 'moron'.

Just then Harry and Burnt Offering came up and lifted out the picnic hampers, that contained the lunches, as though they were as light as a feather.

The 'Redcar Racegoers' took their packed lunches, which consisted of smoked salmon sandwiches, nuts and crisps, a bit of salad, pork pies, sausage rolls, an apple and an orange. "Look at this lot" Bert was heard to say, "it's just like Christmas when I was a lad – nuts and crisps and an apple and an orange as well – that's what we used to have in our stockings"

Elizabeth replied, "I don't care to hear about you dressing up in women's clothes, thank you very much!"

To which Bert was about to remonstrate that she had misunderstood about the stockings when the General said, "leave it Bert. You know what these old biddies are like sometimes, just walk away and we'll get off to the races."

The racegoers picked up their packed lunches and headed off ostensibly to the far end of the beach to find a spot to eat them. Harry and Terry had organised a mini-bus that would whisk them all away to Redcar which he'd booked in advance. The group of racegoers which included Eric, who was desperately trying to get away from sandwich distribution duties, and Burnt Offering made up the staffing contingent.

So this Redcar faction consisted of Harry, The General, Bert, Gertie, Terry, Peggy, Burnt Offering and Eric. A total of eight people all together, just right for the Mercedes people carrier they'd booked. It was about three quarters of an hour to Redcar being approximately twenty odd miles away.

The General took charge of rounding people up and cajoling them to get a bit of a move on as he didn't want to miss the first race. "You can eat those in the mini-bus" he was saying to Gertie and Terry just as they were about to stop and open up their packed lunches, "come along now everybody, chop, chop."

The Remainers in Whitby, as they were called, were still getting off the coach and meandering around the car park in a sort of daze. The racegoers were halfway along the front and, going the other way, was the group going to Robin Hood's Bay who had also managed to retrieve their packed lunches and discreetly slip away.

Harry had arranged to drive the mini-bus, people carrier, because he wasn't that big a drinker during the daytime and so was quite happy to drive. It was virtually compulsory that when going to the races it was almost always accompanied by the consumption of copious amounts of alcohol. The other members of this excursion had come prepared; – the General and Bert both had their hip flasks generously filled with whisky; Terry'd bought a couple of half bottles of gin for, his grandmother, Gertie, and for her friend Peggy and he, Terry, Burnt Offering and Eric were all drinking Guinness initially from the cans stowed away on the coach and later provided on site in the inevitable 'Guinness Tent'. Terry remarked to Eric that Guinness was good for all sorts of ailments and Eric asked "How come?"

To which Terry replied, "well you drink eight pints of this and then you really don't feel a thing."

The journey there was pretty uneventful, other than the frequency of toilet stops. It was not only the General and Bert, who were expected to require frequent stops, but also Eric, Burnt Offering and Terry due to the amounts of Guinness being consumed en-route.

The first race was at 13:30 and so they had to get a bit of a move on although Harry's driving was much better than Del's. They arrived in the car park just after one o'clock, paid for their entrance and immediately made for the toilets again. Harry procured the race cards so that they could all continue to study the form. This resulted in a certain amount of fairly heated banter regarding which horses should be backed.

Bert was saying, "no, you need an outsider in the first race, it's always the way."

The General nodded and said rather gruffly, "we need some cast iron tips here you know. I'm not made of money."

Harry was suggesting they 'play it safe' whilst Terry and Eric had a rather heated argument, mainly fuelled by the Guinness. Eric said, "I know it's twenty five to one but this horse has a good trainer and it's definitely worth an each way bet!"

Terry looked at his mobile phone and Eric said, "are you checking it out?"

To which Terry replied, "no, I've just received a text from Santa, saying that he is real after all."

"Well you back what you like then if you're going to be funny about it," said Eric.

"Oh, I will, don't you worry about that," said Terry decisively.

Eventually they all managed to get their bets on the first race and stood near the finishing post for the best view of the horses as they approached the final straight.

Harry, Terry and Eric all stood together being a lot younger than the others and as the race started, Terry was shouting out his horses name and smacking his bottom like what children do after they've been watching a cowboy film. As the race progressed towards its climax the smacking got more and more frantic and the shouting got louder and louder and just at that point Terry fell over.

Eric looked down at him and said, "well you ran a good race Terry, but you fell at the last."

Everyone laughed as the General and Bert went off to pick up their winnings leaving Gertie and Peggy to wonder what had gone wrong with their selections.

As the afternoon wore on nearly everyone was a winner, backing at least one horse that came first, or in the first three, if it was an each-way bet. All had won something except Burnt Offering who 'hadn't broken the ice yet' to use the expression when a person hasn't had a win or a place all afternoon. Many of the bets were what is known as an 'each way bet' meaning that if the horse wins or is second or third then they should at least get some money back. For second or third places it's only a proportion of the odds but if the horse is an outsider, with long odds, even place money is well worth having.

Burnt Offering was mumbling to himself and getting more and more aggressive. He had foolishly devised a system for 'doubling up' so that after each loss he would double his stake for the next race in the hope of winning back previous losses.

Harry was very comfortable with his wins and had a pile of cash in his pocket and of course was discreet and also conscious of the fact that he had to work at the same place as Burnt Offering and so just grunted non-committal sounds when anyone asked him how he was doing. Eric and Terry on the other hand went over the top bragging about their winnings and ostentatiously started buying drinks all round for their little group.

This made Burnt Offering even angrier and Terry and Eric couldn't resist winding him up further by saying such things as "not another loser" and "you couldn't pick your nose, you couldn't, let alone winners."

Burnt Offering's cheekbones were glowing bright red at this stage which might have something to do with the amount of beer he'd drunk but more likely reflected the anger simmering just below the surface. He was almost pulsating like some machine warning system about to go critical.

Harry had seen the signs before and warned Terry and Eric to keep their distance as they went off to place their bets for the last race. He said, "if Bur….. Tony…. looses it then it'll be like a supernova exploding star – you'll see it coming but there's nothing you can do about it!"

THE OUTING

Peggy and Gertie had had a very satisfactory afternoon and picked up three winners and a couple of place bets as well. Peggy kept saying that it would keep 'the wolf away from the door for a little while longer'.

Everyone had placed their bets for the last race and were positioning themselves near the winning post. Burnt Offering seemed to be offering all sorts of promises to some deity or other and the General and Bert were being very analytical about it all. Harry was quietly confident with his selection and Terry and Eric were holding each other up being the worst for wear with all the drink they'd consumed.

When the winning horse romped home Terry and Eric jumped up in the air nearly falling over when they came down and they were shouting and whistling and the nearby crowd were all looking at them. Terry explained breathlessly that they had bet £100 on the nose, £50 each, and the horse that had just won was thirty three to one.

Eric said' "c'mon Terrish lesh gets the winningsh."

"OK," said Terry, "youse gots tha betingsh shlip."

"I ain't got it," said Eric sobering up rather quickly, "youse had it last!"

Terry looked a bit puzzled and said, "no I dain't, youse puts it yours pocketsh see theresh," pointing to Eric's coat pocket.

Eric turned the inside of his pocket out wards but there's no sign of a betting slip anywhere.

"What'll we do?" said Terry.

Eric put his arm around Terry's shoulder and said, "everyone's should believe in shomething," and Terry nodded as Eric continued, "so I belivesh I'll have ahnother drink!"

With that they both walked off laughing having lost a betting slip worth well over three thousand pounds.

Burnt Offering was by now incandescent with rage not only

because he hadn't won a sausage all afternoon but also because those two buffoons, as he called them, could laugh about losing a winning betting slip. No one dared to approach him and Harry tentatively suggested that they should be getting back to Whitby for the fish and chip supper.

They all piled back into the minibus for the return journey back to Whitby. As there was still some booze left from earlier they carried on drinking with Eric and Terry getting even more drunk. The General and Bert had exhausted their hip flasks but as there was a bottle of Johnnie Walker on board they also carried on imbibing. Gertie and Peggy were the only ones reasonably sober and that was only because sometimes the booze interfered with their medication either making it more potent or rendering it less intoxicating. Nevertheless Peggy and Gertie were doing a considerable amount of damage to a bottle of Bombay Sapphire Gin that they'd found from somewhere and it was fortunate that Harry had seen fit to provide a stock of tonics to go with it.

CHAPTER 14

Robin Hood's Bay

The Robin Hood's Bay group were planning to hire a taxi to take them the five or six miles from Whitby to the Bay. As they needed a taxi for eight people they needed a mini-bus similar to the Redcar group but complete with a driver rather than self-drive which is what the racegoers had.

In spite of Rebecca's insistence that there was no Robin Hood, her grandmother Elizabeth was convinced otherwise. The others all thought she'd been watching too much TV and Beryl, Mary and Cyril were under the impression that it might be The Robin Hood pub that Elizabeth was referring to being the sort of traditional pub which served traditional drinks and snacks.

The group had split up with Elizabeth, Rebecca and Old Joe going one way and Mary, Beryl and Cyril going the other way. Mo and Priya decided to stay where they were and finish off their lunches whilst sitting on some deck chairs that they'd acquired. So the groups wondered up and down the front, one lot looking for a pub and the others looking for a legend.

Mary, Beryl and Cyril were soon worn out and as they were looking for a pub Cyril reasoned that one pub was pretty much as good as another and so kept suggesting different pubs that they passed. The problem was that Mary was so incredibly indecisive and having walked the length of the bay this sub group couldn't find the Robin Hood pub and so, as they were tired, Cyril was suggesting a modern looking pub that they had stopped outside off for a rest. Mary was saying, "let's go in there," then after a pause would say, "no as you were, we'll look for somewhere else," and then, "oh, this will do won't it?"

Cyril and Beryl looked at her in amazement before Beryl took control and said, "I'm not walking another inch without a drink and so we're going in there," and forcibly added, "are you coming in Cyril?"

Mary followed them in and Cyril and Beryl ordered the local craft beer that this pub brewed out the back in their brewing yard. Being local and craft meant that it was extraordinarily strong. Beryl said that she didn't normally drink beers but was thirsty and therefore needed a long drink. Mary was still trying to make up her mind what to have and Cyril and Beryl had finished their drinks and ordered two more. In the end Mary eventually decided to join them and despatched a glass of the local strong ale fairly swiftly. After a few more drinks none of them were very steady on their feet which they all thought was pretty funny really for no apparent reason.

Meanwhile Elizabeth, Rebecca and Old Joe had walked the length and breadth of the bay and Rebecca had finally convinced Elizabeth to have a break funnily enough in the same pub that Cyril, Beryl and Mary were in. As Old Joe went to go to the bar, at first he couldn't make out very much at all because it was quite dark inside, but then he spotted the other three and called to Elizabeth and Rebecca to go and join the others and he would bring the drinks over.

There was faux brasses and traditional pub décor and artefacts which didn't quite work with the overall theme of the pub as it was quite modern. It was really a pretty basic watering hole and specialised in the 'wet trade' rather than offering much in the way of food. It looked as though several refurbishments had been attempted but all they had done was temporarily smarten up what was essentially a bit of shabby pub. There were the inevitable groups of regulars who looked at the latest batch of newcomers arrivals in silence and then got on with their drinking.

Cyril then made his way to the bar and managed to order a round of drinks. It was pints all round regardless of the protests made by Elizabeth and Rebecca. The six of them then started to compare their experiences of Robin Hood's Bay. Mary was making very little sense and Beryl was punctuating every other word with enough expletives to make even Cyril blush.

Mary said to Cyril, "why do you drink so much Cyril? Most evenings you seem to be having a drink back at the Home and so you must drink quite a bit?"

Cyril thought for a minute and replied, "I dunno really Mary, it's one of life's great mysteries that is."

Mary continued, "well haven't you ever tried going 'on the wagon'?"

"I did try it once and it was one of the longest days of my life, to paraphrase Humphrey Bogart. And I suppose that I just fell off again. But the fiddle, sorry deal, that me and Eric made with the 'poncey wine clubs' means that we have a ready source of quality booze and cheap too and so whilst it's there we might as well indulge as it were."

As the afternoon wore on it became evident, they reasoned through their drunken fuzziness, that they were in a pub on their own, without supervision. It was a peculiar feeling because, other than Rebecca, they always had carers on hand to help them. If they had not been so drunk they may have been a bit concerned about getting back to Whitby and more importantly when their next medications were due.

Through a considerable beery haze Cyril was trying to articulate their predicament, "itshh time we's were gettings bak y'know?"

The others looked at him as though he was from another planet and Beryl came out with such an amount of verbal abuse which stunned the rest of the group into silence. They all sat there thinking that really they ought to be doing something like trying to find their way back to Whitby. But it just wouldn't come, the dots didn't join up and so they sat there staring into space. Mary mumbled to herself that sometimes the hamster fell asleep at the wheel which the others just about heard and they all thought it was an incredibly witty thing to say.

The basic problem for a group of elderly people at Robin Hood's Bay is that it is a bay and other than walking from one side of the bay to the other there isn't a lot to do. It's an old fishing village and has a large sandy beach and rock pools which is ideal for families but not so good for pensioners who aren't too sound on their pins.

This hadn't perturbed Elizabeth though as she was convinced she would be meeting Robin Hood in person even though Rebecca had kept trying to get through to her that there wasn't going to be a Robin Hood to meet. However once in the pub all of this was soon forgotten and after a couple of pints they began to wonder why they'd come to the bay in the first place.

Priya and Mo were just glad to get away from the other staff and only have a few of the inmates to look after. They kept an eye on them as their little group seemed to be breaking up into two different factions. The inmates seemed to be going for walks and looked to be fine and so, once the lunches were finished, Mo and Priya thought they would close their eyes for a second or two, just to rest them for a bit.

Several hours later when Mo and Priya awoke with something of a start as the sun had gone in and it had started to cloud over. They both looked around trying to reorient themselves and eventually realising what had happened they started to look for the others.

Mo said, "we need to find them soon because we have their medications that they'll need to take."

"I know," said Priya, "I wonder where they could have got to"

"Let's try along the front a little way. They may have ducked into one of the pubs when it started to cloud over," suggested Mo.

As they strolled along the front the weather started to brighten up again and Mo and Priya quite enjoyed walking along the bay. Although there was still no sign of their little group and they were beginning to get quite concerned.

Priya said, "I can't see them along here anyway and to be quite honest I could do with a drink, I'm parched. Do you think we could pop into this pub and have a lemonade or something?"

"Yeah, let's do that. It sounds like someone's enjoying themselves in there," said Mo as the sound of singing reached their ears. By chance they both entered the very same pub the others were in which was hardly surprising in a way as it was a large pub and fairly prominent amongst other buildings along the front.

"Someone sounds very jolly," went on Mo as they entered the rather dark pub to the sound of a good old sing-song going on.

Priya listened and said, "I think someone's had one or two over the odds."

As they turned towards the bar, there on their left, in one of the booths was Elizabeth, Rebecca, Mary, Beryl, Old Joe and Cyril. All six of them were singing their hearts out in spite of repeated appeals from the landlord that they weren't licensed for music. Not that most people would have likened the cat wailing singing, they were belting out, to music.

Mo said to Priya, "if he calls that music he must be tone deaf!"

Priya just nodded and went over to the very drunken group who were by now having trouble with their harmonies.

"Having a nice time, are we?" said Priya.

Cyril thought very carefully about this and said, "yeashh."

Mo said that she would go and get a drink for her and Priya and ignored the calls from the others for six more pints of the potent craft beer that they had all been drinking.

Mo retuned with two lemonades for her and Priya and said, "I don't think we should be giving them any medication now. Not with all the booze they've drunk. I think we'll have to see how they are after they've had their fish and chip supper in Whitby. Talking of which we'll need to get this lot moving soon."

Mo and Priya were relieved because they thought that they had 'lost' their little unofficial sub-group.

Mo said, "You lot had us worried for a while then, we thought we'd lost you"

"Piss Off!" shouted Beryl as the whole pub stopped and looked.

"Shhhhh…." said Cyril, "dos yousesh want to ghet us cuck…. chuck….thrown out?"

"I'd likesh toos sees themss try it," slurred Beryl who didn't so much sit down as collapse on the seating nearly toppling the table. "Anyways," she continued "you shound like a chicken, you dos with all this chuck, chucl, chuck…..ing!"

At this point the Landlord could see that there was trouble brewing. 'Just what I need,' he thought, 'a load of geriatric hooligans.'

The Landlord walked up to their table and said, "Come on you lot, I think you've had enough. Haven't you got homes to go to?"

Beryl, Mary and Cyril found this hilarious and started laughing whilst Elizabeth and Rebecca were smiling with rather vacant looks in their eyes. Old Joe slurred, "not homeshh but Home! We's alls live together."

"Yeah in a Yellow Submarine," finished Beryl and guffawed.

Mo and Pryia said that they were trying to get them back to Whitby and the Landlord kindly agreed to phone for a taxi to take them away.

CHAPTER 15

Meanwhile back in Whitby

The Matron, Nurse Brown and Brenda, and what later became more widely known as the Remainers group were packing up their deck chairs and putting back on shoes and socks. The most adventurous of the group had managed a paddle after lunch.

The Remainers group included Young Joe, Soups Baxter and Big and Little Johns amongst others and together with Derick and Wayne they had initially remained in Whitby since the coach dropped them off at mid-day. This didn't mean that the group stayed together and some had opted for deck chairs and the beach and others a stroll around the harbour and pier or the town itself.

Matron had asked them who would like to go to the Museum or the photography exhibition and initially there hadn't been many takers. As the afternoon wore on however, it had started to cloud over and so most of the Remainers decided to go and have a look. She handed out the tickets and decided that she would go with them whilst Nurse Brown stayed with those that were quite content on the beach sleeping in their deck chairs.

As they approached the Museum, Soups was more than a little bit nervous as he'd forged all of the tickets. He was thinking to himself that he wished that they'd had a more recent ticket to copy from. In the event he needn't have worried as the pensioner concessions meant that they did not need the tickets in the end.

The Victorian Museum at Whitby contains a collection of old

fossils and Matron thought she better keep her little group moving in case they ended up being mistaken for relics themselves. It was difficult to manage, as the inmates wondered off in various directions looking at the different exhibits.

Matron said, "come along now. Who would like to see the model ships?"

There was general mumbling, "Who wants to see model ships," and, "I've had enough of ships to last me a lifetime," and so on.

"Well how about the natural history exhibits, they look interesting, don't they?" Matron asked.

"Suppose so," mumbled a couple of the inmates, others were saying that they would rather be down the pub!

"Great," she thought out loud, "They're about as enthusiastic as turkeys at Christmas time," and "I wonder what happened to Gertie, Elizabeth and some of the others? The carers have also gone off somewhere and left me and Nurse Brown to deal with those remaining at Whitby."

Meanwhile, Derick had decided to get the brakes checked on the coach as he wasn't happy with them. This made Wayne doubly unhappy because he had to go with him instead of chasing after some of the young girls that seemed to be in abundance in the town. Wayne also thought that it wouldn't be necessary to get the brakes checked if it wasn't for Derick's erratic driving which was totally inconsistent and therefore required excessive use of the brakes.

Wayne could tell it was going to cost a lot when the mechanic at the garage that they took the coach too started tutting and sighing and generally shaking his head and sucking his teeth. "never mind the theatrics," said Wayne, "how much is it going to cost?"

"Well," said the mechanic shaking his head some more, "when the brakes are abused like this, it's not only the brake pads, but also discs and drums that should be replaced."

"Just replace the pads, OK?" said Wayne whilst Derick tried to but in to get him to agree to changing the discs and drums as well.

The mechanic said, "well Ok then but really the lot needs to be replaced. Who's been driving this thing?"

"He has," said Wayne, indicating Derick with his head.

Derick butted in and said, "well there is such a lot of idiots on the roads these days isn't there? Some of them drive so slow that I'm always putting the brakes on. Then there are the maniacs who drive too fast and, I'm worried about them as well, and so I brake to let them overtake. I tell you the roads are full of idiots and maniacs. Why can't they all drive like me?"

Wayne looked at Derick amazed at what he'd just heard and said, "if they all drove like you we'd never get anywhere and there'd be so many crashes that the roads would just seize up. We'll replace the pads for now and when we get back to the depot we'll get the brakes looked at properly."

The mechanic bristled a bit at that and shrugged his shoulders and said, "well it's your funeral mate," and walked off to get the parts.

Wayne said to Derick, "you stay here and keep an eye on him and make sure he does a good job!"

"But I ain't got any money to pay him," moaned Derick.

"Here, this is the company credit card, - I'll write the PIN on your hand -don't wash it off before you've paid!"

Wayne headed back into the town centre to chance his luck with some of the young ladies although in his case he believed he was irresistible and so luck didn't come into it.

Those of the Remainers group that had not gone to the Museum, had not been incident free and this group had also included Kevin the Klepto who had 'gone shopping'. No one knew why he pinched the things he did, he certainly didn't need them. But he would go into a supermarket or newsagents and appropriate chocolate, sweets, cakes, biscuits, - whatever he could get his hands on really. It wasn't that he was hungry but he liked the shiny wrappings and wanted to keep them, which he usually did until way past their sell by dates.

Kevin was currently being chased down the road by an irate shopkeeper. Unfortunately he was going away from the group he'd been with. They'd all stopped what they were doing and watched and one or two started shouting odds of him getting away. Most thought he would be caught. However after a nifty bit of ducking and diving, Kevin managed to disappear in the crowds of people milling about and the Remainers group were wondering if he would be able to find his way back when two more of their group came staggering up.

'The Johns', as they were known, consisted of Little John, who was an unrepentant flasher and Big John, who would egg him on. Big John's party piece was that he was into mooning. So one flashed at the front and the other flashed at the back so to speak. They had discovered the stash of booze on the coach which was supposed to be for on the way back. But niceties like that didn't bother them and they got stuck in. Once the booze took hold they just couldn't help themselves and would drop their trousers faster than you could say 'here's a policeman' which usually stopped them in their tracks.

Brenda was busy helping Nurse Brown get the Remainers settled and none of them had noticed the disappearance of the little sub-groups to the races and Robin Hood's Bay. Also the mischievous comings and goings of Kevin the Klepto and the two Johns had gone unnoticed until now.

Nurse Brown had missed all the excitement of the visit to the museum and the antics of Kevin and the John's mainly because of Young Joe. Young Joe, who was usually quiet and hardly said a word, currently had a touch of the verbal diarrhoeas. Although well into his eighties he was trying earlier to chat up Nurse

Brown much to the disgust of Matron. Young Joe had managed to have a drink with his lunch and as he was already taking a potent mix of tablets he was actually as high as a kite.

Nurse Brown was trying to be polite and fend him off but he was very persistent and in the end Matron had to step in, on her return from the Museum, and threaten enemas and all sorts of treatments to get him to back off.

Young Joe eventually moved off and tried chatting up Brenda instead. Brenda thought it best to humour him and so had a drink or two with him until he got bored and wondered off. Young Joe used to joke that he still liked to chase women but that he didn't know what to do with them once he caught them now!

The majority of the Remainers were no trouble, at least initially, and having departed the coach they'd set about acquiring deck chairs. The first challenges came in trying to set up the deck chairs, of course, which seemed to have a mind of their own. When they were eventually set up some of them collapsed moments later to great hoots of laughter.

Finally they all had seats and managed to eat their packed lunches sitting down. A few had got the odd bottle of beer, that had been secreted on the coach by Harry and Eric, and so they all enjoyed their lunches and one or two thought they would have another beer and then another until they eventually fell asleep.

Others were quite happy messing about on the beach and wandered off to build sandcastles or do a bit of paddling in the sea. The weather was initially sunny and warm and so they all enjoyed the seaside. Of course being the British seaside the weather is never that reliable and as the afternoon wore on it became more changeable and clouded over from time to time. Not that many of the inmates noticed as they were either too engrossed in what they doing or sleeping. Others were slightly the worse for drink and so they just didn't care one way or the other.

The visit to the Museum hadn't been the success that they had anticipated and when this little group returned they discovered that there had been booze on the coach and so they thought they would have a few before their fish and chips.

So the Remainers enjoyed a relatively calm afternoon other than the antics of Kevin and the Johns. It did start to occur to Matron and Nurse Brown as the afternoon wore on that some of the inmates had gone off to 'do their own thing' as someone had said. This confirmed Matron's suspicions and she wasn't very pleased about being kept in the dark about these unauthorised excursions.

CHAPTER 16

Fish and Chip Suppers for All

As the Remainers group started to come together, getting ready for the fish and chips before heading back to the Home, it was noted that there were considerably less inmates than when they arrived. This sparked some concern from Nurse Brown who said, "where have all the others got to? I can't see them anywhere on the beach."

Matron took control and said, "Oh they're probably gone up into the town looking at the shops. I overheard some snippets that a few had gone off, 'doing their own thing', I think they'd said. I think they'll be OK because the carers seem to have gone with them and Kevin the Klepto remained here with the Johns – who are about the biggest troublemakers we have!"

She then looked a bit uncertain and added, "actually I think Kevin went off somewhere earlier. I just hope he's keeping out of trouble, and come to think of it, I haven't seen the Johns lately either!"

Nurse Brown said, "I don't remember seeing Kevin, if he's gone off somewhere chances are he's up to no good and he's probably in a police station by now."

Matron said, "well, there's nothing more we can do about it just now. If we don't get this lot their fish and chip suppers we'll be in trouble so we'd better sort this out first."

The Fish and Chip suppers had already been pre-ordered from

Hadleys on Bridge Street. These fish and chips were considered to be amongst the finest in Whitby. There was a restaurant and also a takeaway service. The Remainers all started to line up to collect their fish and chips. Once they had collected them they moved to the benches on the pier to eat them.

It was all going fine until the Redcar racegoers group arrived. They were all inebriated, except Harry, and they were singing very loudly as they approached the back of the queue.

Matron and Nurse Brown told them to be quiet as they waited to be served to which there were giggles, laughter and a lot of hiccups. Matron said to Harry, "where have you been? We've not seen hide nor hair of you since we arrived at lunchtime."

Harry just shrugged and replied, "a few of us thought a trip to the races at Redcar would be good and so myself and Eric arranged for a mini-bus to take a few of the inmates who are keen on horse racing."

"Well you should have cleared it with me first!" said Matron looking around for Brenda for a bit of moral support.

Harry looked at her and, as fierce as she was, he stood up to her and said, "I don't recall being subject to your supervision. I'm in charge of maintenance and Eric is in charge of the carers. If we want to organise a little extra activity then we are quite within our rights to do so without asking your permission."

Matron glowered at him and shouted, "look here you jumped up little handy man. I'm not interested in what low life's like you and Eric think! In future you will tell me about such things. I have overall responsibility for these people and I expect you to help me look after them. Do I make myself clear?"

"Look Matron, you might have had a hard day terrorising the inmates but don't think you can lord it over me or Eric," said Harry.

Matron was rapidly reaching boiling point, and her face was going through a series of colours ranging from incandescent white to an explosive shade of red, when Burnt Offering arrived on the scene. Harry inwardly winced as Burnt Offering started slurring in broad Glaswegian. No one could understand him when he was talking with such a broad Scottish accent and especially when he was drunk to boot. Even Eric, who was as drunk as Burnt Offering couldn't make out what he was saying.

Matron said, "you're a raging drunk!"

To which Burnt Offering took a deep breath and replied in almost coherent English, "Ifs youse can findsh a taxi…taxi…taxidermist willings to undertakes th' work – Git Stuffed!"

Matron bellowed, "I've never been so insulted in my life!"

Harry, Eric and Burnt Offering all replied in unison, "you must have been!"

Matron stormed off shouting over her shoulder that they could sort out the fish and chips for their lot themselves while she went back to attend to the Remainers a few more of which had turned up to watch the row going on. She wanted to find Brenda and get her help in controlling this drunken rabble.

The Redcar racegoers joined the back of the queue and were basically propping each other up like pairs of bookends. There was the General and Bert, Gertie and Peggy, Eric and Terry with Burnt offering sort of leaning on both of them.

Harry said, "OK, try and look as sober as you can. This is the queue for the fish and chips…."

"chish and fips," said the General and everybody howled with laughter.

Harry said, "just try and keep as straight a line as you can till you've got served and then you can go over towards the pier, there's a few benches there to sit on."

The little group looked at Harry like he was some sort of demigod and tried to nod their heads but as this produced a bit too much dizziness and so they were content to just give rather gormless looks coupled with the occasional giggling and burping.

The Remainers continued to be served and the queue moved forward and just as the Redcar racegoers were about to launch into a resounding chorus of "why are we waiting" the Robin Hood's Bay group arrived. This group was even more pissed than the racegoers if that was possible and again they were beginning to get a bit belligerent because they hadn't had a drink for all of five minutes.

Once again Matron came storming up, "and where the devil have you been may I ask?"

Old Joe took a deep breath and managed to say, "you may," without slurring.

"Ashhk awayhh," said Elizabeth currently being supported by her granddaughter, Rebecca, who herself was struggling to stay upright and keep a straight face.

"Well? Where have you been?" said Matron.

"Here, there and everywhere," sang Elizabeth as she burst into an old Beatles song and was quickly joined by the others from the Robin Hood's Bay group.

"Quiet!" she shouted, "I've not seen you lot since we arrived so I'll ask again; where have you been? Mo, Priya what have you been up to with this little lot?" Matron demanded.

"We've been a little way along the coast to Robin Hood's Bay," said Mo and Priya nodded adding, "it was only just up the coast and we didn't think that anyone would mind."

"Who gave you permission to take these people away from the main group? That's what I'd like to know!" Matron continued, her colour, just beginning to return to normal, took on a reddish hue once more.

Mo and Priya gathered their little group around them mistakenly thinking that a safety in numbers approach might placate Matron and Mo said, "we only went a little way along the coast and knew that we would be back for the fish and chips and so we just went, didn't we." The group were all vigorously nodding their heads which was a mistake in Beryl's case because she fell over.

Mo and Priya helped Beryl up and looked at Matron who was approaching nuclear fall-out status at this stage.

"Didn't it occur to you to let us know where you going? Honestly sometimes I don't think you've got the brains you were born with. Anything could have happened," said Matron exasperatedly.

"Nows then don't, don't youse gets hhaving a go at themsh," slurred Elizabeth, "itsh wash my ideah and I'll take fullsh responsibility……"

"You have no responsibility to take you silly woman," interrupted Matron.

"Now look here Matron," started Old Joe being physically held up by Cyril. If he continued to take deep breaths he could just about talk without slurring his words and more importantly without falling over. He said, "just because we've gone off the reservation a bit……," interrupted by hoots of laughter……," doesn't mean to say we've been up to no good, does it?"

Matron glowered at him and said, "yes it does you stupid, drunk little man!"

Old Joe took another deep breath and said, "now wait a minute Matron, that's a bit strong isn't it?"

"Oh, for goodness sake, get in the queue, you horrible person, for your fish and chips," said Matron, "and make sure you're at the coach on time otherwise we'll go without you!"

Brenda had heard the commotion going on with Matron as the Redcar group and the Robin Hood's Bay group returned and thought it best if she stayed well out of it. She'd manage to get in quickly and have her fish and chips and so she went off in search of the coach with the intention of perhaps returning with it to pick them all up instead of having them wander around Whitby looking for it or more likely looking for another drink or getting up to further mischief.

Eventually all of the inmates got served and moved off onto the pier or elsewhere to eat the fish and chips. It was a bit risky having the fish and chips, considering the amount of booze some of them had consumed, but they all managed to keep the food down without being sick. They all slowly ambled back to the coach which of course was not where it had been left because Derick had had to get the brake pads changed.

It was a sight to behold as a couple of dozen geriatrics tried to rationalise where the coach had gone, the rationale for the missing coach became more outlandish once the ones that had been drinking started on trying to find out where it was.

"It's gone without us," said Mary sounding reasonably sober.

"Mary, were all here how could it go without us?" replied Elizabeth who had also come round a bit after her fish and chips.

"It's a bad show," said the General beginning to sober up as well.

Brenda had looked all over the car park and couldn't find the coach and as the others arrived said, "I've looked everywhere for it but I don't know where it's got to!"

A little crowd of inmates had gathered round her and started mumbling about getting back to the Home. Matron, Nurse Brown and a few more joined them and Matron said, "well this just isn't good enough. We left the coach just about there," pointing to an empty coach space, "but where it is now, God only knows!"

As soon as Matron had said this a few of the inmates immediately broke into the Beach Boys song of 'God Only Knows' and were singing at the top of their voices much to the amusement of passers-by.

There was a lot of shaking of heads and more mumblings about things not being reliable as in 'my day' as they started to split up and look for the coach in a sort of half-hearted manner.

Whilst all this tooing and froing of looking for the coach was going on, Eric and Terry and Cyril and Bert took it into their heads to go off and ransack an off-licence. A similar thought had occurred to Tom Soups Baxter and Old Joe because most of the booze for consumption on the return trip had now been drunk. There were several off-licences just up from the High Street and Eric and Terry selected the first one they came to leaving Cyril and Bert and Soups and Old Joe to go a bit further afield.

The ploy was simple enough, mainly to buy some bottles of beer and to acquire wine as spirits as best they could which translated meant 'knock off' the wine and spirits. This was no easy feat as most spirits are stored behind the counters. So the idea was to buy whatever they couldn't acquire easily and to purloin the rest.

Eric had most of his and Harry's floats and Cyril had managed to get Mo and Priya to let him have what was left of their floats on the proviso he bought some snacks for the coach journey back to the Manor.

Soups and Old Joe had their own money, both still earning as it were, and they chose the off-licence furthest away thinking that this would preserve their anonymity. This nearly backfired as they were spotted trying to force a bottle of gin under Soups's jumper. But they had only got as far as a few bottles of wine and so were able to move pretty quickly and soon lost any chance of a pursuit by going down a series of backstreets. The fact that they ended up lost was a minor consideration. Still they thought the excitement of the chase was worth it and they did eventually find their way back to the coach park.

Cyril and Bert managed to get hold of some bottles of beer which were heavy and so they weren't really able to acquire much else. Cyril said, "why don't we get the cans of beer and, that way we can carry more, been as they're not so heavy?"

Bert said, "no, I don't care for canned beer. It always tastes tinny to me. We'll stick to bottles for us I think."

Meanwhile Eric and Terry had scored a bumper haul of wine, beer and spirits. They'd spent all of the floats and had acquired a few of what they termed 'freebies' and were struggling under the weight to get it back to the coach. In the end they had to flag down a taxi and just as the taxi pulled into the coach park Derick arrived with the coach explaining about the repairs that had been necessary.

The small groups and individuals all started to migrate towards the coach; Soups and Old Joe came running up looking a bit flushed from the exertion of running and carrying their haul, Kevin the Klepto similarly darted up and pushed forward so as to get on the coach before the others, Eric and Terry recruited some of the others to help them load up the booze onto the coach.

Mo and Priya were a bit put out that there was no change from Cyril and Bert and as Mo said, "and where's the bloody snacks then?"

"Oh we didn't get chance to get them," said Cyril, "we were in the off-licence and we saw the coach come past and so we thought we'd get back sharpish – which is why we were running," he lied.

Mo and Priya shrugged and shook their heads in such a way as to make it clear that they didn't believe a word they were saying. Mo said to Priya , "I think we deserve a drink after the way Matron spoke to us earlier."

"Too right," said Priya, "I mean who does she think she is. Eric's our boss not her and I intend to put a dent in that booze the inmates have brought back!"

CHAPTER 17

The Return Journey – Homeward Bound

Derick had paid the mechanic using Wayne's corporate credit card and attempted to return to the coach park where he had previously parked only to find that it was full to capacity. He then decided to drive to an out-of-town parking area and wait there until the time came to collect the Manor's Outing group. Unfortunately he couldn't remember what time he was supposed to pick them up. Wayne always dealt with that side of things and as there was no sign of Wayne and so Derick thought he ought to go and look for him.

So as the afternoon had worn on Derick had looked for Wayne but to no avail. He then thought that it must be close enough to pick-up time by now and that there should be an empty parking bay available at this time and so off he went.

Meanwhile Wayne had completely lost track of time and had found himself in a wine bar trying to chat up a couple of local girls who he was plying with drink in the hope of getting off with one or both of them.

Wayne had very little idea about how to treat women and was using chat up lines his grandfather would have used such as;

"Did it hurt?"

To which the young lady would respond, "did what hurt?"

Wayne, "when you fell from heaven."

Now most young ladies thought this a bit morbid with the falling from heaven line a bit like what might happen when someone dies and so it usually didn't go over at all well and the girls in Whitby were no exception to this.

So Wayne had spent most of the afternoon drinking and buying drinks for girls who had much better things to do and so didn't stay too long.

Eventually it dawned on him that he had a job to do in rounding up the 'geriatrics' as he called them and getting them on the coach back to the Manor Home. He reluctantly started towards where he thought the coach would be parked but got lost and couldn't remember exactly where it was. Being too proud to ask for directions he'd wandered around the town until he eventually spotted Kevin running one way and then Cyril and Bert running in another direction and then Eric and Terry. He was turning his head this way and that in a most comical manner when Soups and Old Joe came across him and Soups said, "you don't want to stand here all day looking gormless you know, we've got to get back on the coach, or you'll be left behind!"

Wayne reluctantly followed them to the coach park and shouted after them, "our coach company never leaves anyone behind!" He added, "We're like the SAS in that way."

This was lost on Soups and Old Joe who just wanted to get back to deposit their booze onto the coach.

Derick had started to get the inmates on board and the coach was about half full when Wayne eventually got to it and he was surprised by the amount of booze on board although he didn't really need any more to drink having been drinking all afternoon.

Again after a lot more tooings and froing's, the staff and inmates were settled into their seats ready for the off. Wayne tried to count the numbers but as he'd lost his earlier count from when they arrived he'd no idea what number he needed to back into. After three attempts, and three different numbers, Wayne went up and down the coach looking at the empty seats and saying, "is there anyone sitting here?"

To which the replies varied from 'piss off' to 'no that's alright dear, you can sit there if you want to' and sometimes there was no reply at all because most of the passengers had passed out virtually as soon as they took their seats on the coach. The noise became deafening though as they tried to keep their snoring down to fifty decibels but without much success. Even when Wayne tried to make some announcements it didn't waken them.

The hardened drinkers of course were still going strong and Bert, Cyril, Eric and Old Joe were enjoying the fruits of their shopping expeditions. Harry was attempting to catch up, not having had as much to drink, and Brenda, Mo and Priya were all enjoying what they considered to be a well-earned drink.

As the coach got underway, with Wayne reasoning that it looked like they'd got everybody on board who should be on board, about half were fast asleep and the other half were catching up with the drunks that were still going strong. One or two tried, a bit half-heartedly to get a sing song going with all the songs of the day when they had been young. This consisted of Nelly Dean, Shine on Harvest Moon, a few Vera Lynn classics and 'Somewhere Over the Rainbow' to name just a few.

Old Joe and Young Joe were deep in conversation about the singing, with Young Joe, who was probably the oldest one on the coach saying, "they don't have songs like that anymore."

Old Joe who conversely would have been one of the youngest inmates on the coach said, "I prefer the '60's music, you know the Beatles, The Stones, Manfred Mann and the Kinks. There were so many good bands about in the 1960's, not like now with all this jungle music that they play."

"Oh, I don't like that talking music either." said Young Joe, "that rapping and the shouting and the swearing –it sounds like they're really upset about something but I can't work out what it is because the words are never that clear and I think they also use slang but it's the swearing more than anything that I don't like. What I really like is a bit of a melody with proper signing where you can hear the words and where people actually play their own instruments rather than all this miming that they seem to do now."

Old Joe said, "yeah, I get that, and I don't like this Rap stuff either. In fact most, so called, modern music doesn't seem to have much melody or singing come to that and, as you say, they always seem as though they've got a chip on their shoulder about something or other. I don't know why they need to play it so loud as well. No I don't get that, I mean it almost gives you a nose bleed it's so loud!"

"Sometimes I can hear it in the cars outside," said Young Joe, "it must hurt their ears having it so loud in a confined space like that. You mark my words they'll all be deaf before they're forty!"

"I know," said Old Joe, "I've heard them. When I go out a do a bit of work, there's sometimes this so called 'music' playing which, to me, is just a loud noise, that's all it is, noise. In the sixties they could really belt out a tune with a great melody and beat and didn't need to burst your eardrums to do it. Some of the lyrics could be a bit 'iffy' though," he continued, "I mean there was 'doo wah, diddy diddy' and a few songs with the 'sha la la's' in them.

"They could belt out these old songs that they're singing now as well," said Young Joe referring to Vera Lynn and Judy Garland.

"Yes, I know they could in their day, but what I don't get is why, when people have a sing song, these days, they add an 'a' on the end of everything."

"What do you mean?" said Young Joe.

Old Joe said, "well you listen to them singing 'My Way' just now. They're actually singing 'my-a way-a'. They add an 'a' to the end of the words."

"Oh that's poetic licence, that is. It adds to the expressive nature of the singer," said Young Joe.

"Oh, it's not because they're taking a breath after each word because they're drunk then?" said Old Joe.

"No, no, it wouldn't be that, no, I'm sure it wouldn't be that," said Young Joe rather unconvincingly.

The singing fizzled out after a time because those that knew all of the words started to pass out. This was not only because they'd had a fair bit to drink but also because it was way past their bedtime by now and they were tired out.

Derick was concentrating hard on his driving which even being kind could only be described as erratic. Wayne said to him, "why don't you try and keep up with the flow of traffic, all smooth like, without this constant stopping and starting and jerking the coach around?"

"That's what I'm trying to do, but I've had this maniac following me for the past half hour or so," said Derick.

"That means he's going too fast if he's a maniac, right, "said Wayne.

"Well yes, maniacs do drive too fast, but this car behind me is an idiot as well because he doesn't overtake me he just slows down and come up right close behind me and flashes his lights."

"So he's a maniac and an idiot then," said Wayne, "that's a bit unusual isn't it?"

"It certainly is," moaned Derick braking rather sharply once more.

Wayne was looking out of the back window of the coach and Derick was looking at his rear view mirror when all of a sudden the car behind them came roaring up alongside them with its lights flashing and horn sounding off like some sort of siren.

"What's going on Wayne, what shall I do?" said Derick anxiously, "I think he's trying to board us…"

"Its boats that they board," replied Wayne, "coaches they just hijack." As soon as he said that, Wayne dived down into his seat and tried not to look as the car that had been following them, all this time, suddenly swerved in front of them forcing Derick to stop.

Derick stood on the brakes and squealed to a stop at the side of the road. The car had pulled in at an angle in front of them so that they couldn't continue.

When Wayne saw that it was just a taxi and not an SUV, filled with cutthroats of some sort or another, looking to hijack the coach, he got up and opened the door and shouted, "'ere what's your game? What on Earth do you think you're doing? You nearly ran us off the road!"

The taxi driver was out of his cab and approached Wayne in a menacing manner. Wayne dived back into the coach and said, "I think you need to deal with this Derick, he don't look none too pleased."

The taxi driver climbed the steps and shouted at Derick, "haven't we forgotten something?"

Derick looked at him and was doubly worried, thinking not only is he a maniac and an idiot driver, he's also ready for the funny farm, this one, "forgotten something?" he said alarmed.

"Yes, forgotten something!" repeated the taxi driver.

"No I don't think so," said Derick a bit more puzzled.

Just then out stepped two of the inmates from the back of the taxi, looking a bit worse for wear.

Beryl said to Peggy, "that's one taxi ride I'll never forget!"

"I think I'll need to change my underwear, I don't think I've ever been so frightened with him trying to overtake the coach like that," replied Peggy.

The taxi driver was saying, "I've been following you for miles! Didn't you see me flashing my lights and trying to get your attention?"

Derick said, "well yes, but I thought you were one of those maniacs who just wanted to overtake me and you were just making a meal out of it to show off."

The cabbie shook his head and mumbled something to himself about "don't know where they get them, I really don't"

He looked at Derick and said, "well these two old biddies....."

"Oi, not so much of the old biddy, if you don't mind," shouted out Peggy.

"Sorry, these ladies," he continued looking at Derick, "were left behind! They flagged me down and asked me to catch you up otherwise they didn't know how they were going to get back to the Home. I don't know how you could have left them. Didn't you do a count before you set off?"

"Well……," began Derick, "we … er….. that is……"

"Never mind all that now, I just want my money the ol…… ladies said you'd pay the fare and give me a big tip!"

As the cabbie stood there demanding money from Derick for the taxi ride for Beryl and Peggy, Wayne came up to supposedly sort things out having ascertained that the cabbie did not look like he posed any serious threat.

"What seems to be the problem cabbie?" asked Wayne.

The taxi driver said, "you left them behind and they said that you would pay me and with a big tip if I manged to get them back on the coach!"

Derick shouted, "you'll need to settle up with this bloke, Wayne, because you didn't make sure everybody was back on board when you should have counted them properly!"

Wayne said, "Oh, alright then. How much do I owe you?"

"Its fifty pounds plus tip," said the taxi driver holding out his hand.

Wayne gulped, "how much? I don't have that sort of money on me."

"Well you're not moving this coach until I'm paid," said the taxi driver, "I can stay here all night of necessary!"

Wayne suddenly had an idea and shouted down the coach, "we're having the whip round for the driver now! Please give generously, and give whatever you've got, or we'll never get home tonight."

A few of the inmates had heard the exchange between Wayne and the taxi driver and so they all dug deep and managed to come up with just over £55 plus about ten Euros and a couple of rather optimistic washers.

Wayne handed it over to the cabbie and said, "best we can do, I'm afraid" but as it was mostly in £5 notes and £2 pound coins it looked a lot more than it actually was and so the cabbie reluctantly accepted it and went and moved his cab mumbling all the time about "bloody cowboys giving the transportation industry a bad name."

Wayne and Derick heaved a sigh of relief and closed the door after the cabbie. Wayne shouted down the coach asking if everyone was OK which woke up a few of the inmates and when there were no replies he indicated to Wayne to resume their journey.

Derick said, "you're sure we've got everybody now? You've not left any others behind have you?"

Wayne just shrugged and said, "it's their own fault. I did ask if anyone was missing and nobody replied. I mean what else could I do?"

With that, Derick shook his head and the coach journey resumed.

CHAPTER 18

The return journey continues – second wind - literally

The return journey took forever – mainly due to toilet breaks – no sooner had everyone got back on board than they had to stop again. The inmates would wake up from their sleep, or be woken up because of the noisy snoring, and immediately would want the toilet. Since most of them did not like using the on- board facilities this entailed a stop and then another stop and then another and so on! The amount of booze consumed was also making itself known judging by the chorus of farts taking place. Remarks such as, "it's better out than in," and, "I think it's those mushy peas we had with the fish and chips that are to blame." Needless to say the coach soon began to smell pretty 'sweet'.

When they did stop, it took ages to get people off and back on again and so what would have been a ten minute stop turned into half hour or more and it seemed like five minutes later the whole process had to be repeated again.

The drink that had been brought into the coach continued to be consumed as the inmates gained their second wind after their naps. There was still quite a lot of the booze left and so they just carried on boozing as the coach meandered onwards. Once woken up most of the inmates couldn't then get back to sleep and those that had found their 'second wind' began getting ready to start again with the singing and telling of stories. This inevitably led to some quite heated discussions about essentially trivial matters. Mary, being incredibly indecisive was asked about what epitaph she wanted on her headstone which kicked off quite a heated debate on this fairly morbid topic.

After a somewhat considerable time to ponder the question she said, "Oh, something simple but tasteful would do."

"Do you mean like, 'here lies Mary, quite contrary, didn't want to go, but she went like so!" said Cyril doing his best Tommy Cooper impression.

"No not like that, tasteful I said, but what about you Cyril, what have you got in mind?" asked Mary.

Cyril replied, "well I always liked this little verse;

'When this you see

Remember me,

And keep me in your mind,

Let others say what they may but speak of me as you find'

It sort of sums it up for me because you can't please all the people all of the time can you? How about you Bert what's your epitaph likely to be?"

Bert thought for a minute and said, "well I've not really thought about it but something like, "I told you I wasn't feeling very well," or perhaps, "Science doesn't care what you believe," or even, "no one warned me I was about to exceed the limits of my medication," and he and Cyril both laughed.

Others started to join in this rather morbid topic of conversation with everyone trying to outdo everyone else for the most outlandish epitaphs to put on their headstones.

Tom, Soups Baxter, as he was nicked named, came up with, "I think I'd like, 'none the bloody wiser' on mine!"

Cyril said, "very apt, is that why everyone calls you 'Soups Non the Wiser'?"

"I wasn't aware they did," said Soups rather morosely who could be a bit of a depressive on occasions.

"It's a sort of catch phrase with you Soups," said Cyril, "whenever we ask you something you can provide quite a credible explanation but then you end it all by saying that you are, 'non-the wiser,' which sort of undermines all what you've said."

"Oh," said Soups who decided, at that stage, that looking out of the window would be more interesting and so ignored any further comments on the matter.

Whilst Elizabeth and a couple of the other women thought more traditional, gone but not forgotten, type of memorial words would be more suitable. The men on the other hand thought that something a little bit more unusual would be more in keeping with what they had in mind.

The General suggested, "The supply of curse words was simply insufficient to meet my demands," and laughed.

Old Joe said, "I always knew I'd grow old but I wasn't quite prepared for how quickly it would happen."

"It don't slow down, I can tell you," said the General, "it seems that time accelerates as you get older."

Old Joe continued, "All this talk about getting on, 'climbing the ladder' and such like reminds me of the little ditty about no need to worry. You might remember it? In life there is only ever two things to worry about, whether you are rich or if you are poor. If you are rich you've got nothing to worry about and if you are poor you have two things to worry about. That's whether you're healthy or unhealthy and if you're healthy you've got nothing to worry about and if you are unhealthy you've only got two things to worry about. That's if you are going to live or going to die. If you are going to live then you have nothing to worry about. If you are going to die you've only got two things to worry about. That's if you go up to heaven or down to the other place. If you go to heaven you've got nothing to worry about and if you go down below you'll be that busy shaking hands with all of your friends that you'll have nothing to worry about!"

Gertie decided to chip in by saying, "you know, this getting old malarkey's not for wimps!"

"Whilst we are on the subject what about readings and that. I expect that most of you like me have everything arranged," said Young Joe.

This was a bit close for comfort for some of the inmates of advancing years but Old Joe piped up that he liked 'Turn, Turn, Turn' which was taken from the Bible but had also been a song sung by The Byrds in the 1960s. Another said that they quite liked the 'Reflection on an Autumn Day' reading which was about what a person had made of themselves rather than what possessions they had managed to accumulate.

The General particularly liked that one being very big on character and the rights of the individual. Something he felt strongly about and which he considered had been lacking over the last few years!

"For goodness sake, don't start him off again," pleaded Bert, "I've had all this on the way to Whitby earlier on."

A few of them laughed at this and the things being said, but all this talk of mortality was a sobering thought, and a lot of the inmates started chatting about different things until someone started up the sing-songs again. This time being a little bit more up to date with '60's pop songs and a bit of rock and roll.

Wayne remarked to Derick, "these old 'uns certainly know how to enjoy themselves Del. I hope I'm still rocking and rolling at their age."

Derick just rolled his eyes and waited for the punch line.

Wayne obliged by saying, "I don't think I'll ever get old. I'm mean I'm too good looking to show my age and so I'll be one of those people that go on and on quite merrily until someday I won't, and people will say 'was he really that old – he didn't look it!'. Hopefully though not for a long while yet though eh?"

Derick just shook his head causing the coach to swerve which he just about managed to correct in time.

Most of the inmates were now awake except for those that were really inebriated who were still sleeping it off oblivious to the hair-raising driving of Derick. A few more conversations had started up in between the singing.

Bert and Gertie were having a rather heated conversation about how they were going to spend their winnings with Bert saying that he would be getting a few 'home comforts' whilst Gertie was saying, "but Bert that's your stake for future bets. You can't just squander it!"

Bert said, "I'm not squandering it. I really do need few bits and pieces."

"I'll get Terry to get you what you need. Leave it with me. You can then use your money as part of our syndicate which is far more important. Terry won't charge you very much whatever it is that you need. You know with this sort of stake money we've got we can really go places," said Gertie enthusiastically.

The Redcar racegoers group were still generally celebrating with everyone, except Burnt Offering, taking back quite a bit of money that they had won. Burnt Offering, Tony, was still simmering not so much from not winning but more so for Eric and Terry winding him up about it. He was slowly going ballistic as everyone else was having such a good time going back to the Home on the coach. All he'd done since Redcar was drink himself drunk, then more drunker and then sober and then start all over again! It was not only that he'd drunk himself into a right old state again but more so that he was in such a morose state which was almost bordering on clinical depression. This was not helped by the General keep harping on about stiff upper lip, character and backbone and all that.

Terry suggested that they tie a sign around his neck saying "suicide in progress, do not disturb." But the others thought this might be going a bit too far.

Burnt Offering replied to the General, "No, I don't need anger management, you need to stop pissing me off!"

The General looked a bit 'sheepish' and so turned back to Bert to ask him about the next race meeting they would be betting on.

Terry and Rebecca were chatting about this and that as they steadily got drunk all over again together. Terry said, "to me 'drink responsibly' means don't spill it," as he topped up their glasses again.

Cyril and Beryl were propping each other up on the seat 'spark out'. They were trying to keep the snoring noises down but both of them seemed to be telling themselves stories because every so often they would mumble something and then laugh to themselves. So the volume of singing took on another dimension and the windows on the coach were virtually rattling as the snoring, sleep laughter, talking and singing all reached deafening levels.

Elizabeth said to Mary, "that Tom's a funny bloke you know. He's a good forger and can get you any documents you might need but he keeps going on about being 'non the wiser', miserable old sod."

Mary agreed and said, "he's what they'd call 'not playing with a full deck'."

Elizabeth laughed and said, "my old Mom always used to say people like that were not the full shilling'."

"Or they're a 'sandwich short of a picnic', or a 'firelighter short of a box', or 'they've got a screw loose'." added Mary as they both laughed.

You know a lot of those sayings Mary," said Elizabeth, "I sometimes worry about you, you know?"

Mary replied that she thought it faintly amusing that there were so many sayings for people who might be slightly idiosyncratic. "It's funny that we have these different expressions for people who are not quite normal and yet no one really knows what normal is," she said.

"Just remember Mary," Elizabeth said, "someone once said that life's a tragedy for those who feel and a comedy for those that think."

There were a few nodding their heads at such a profound quote that is until they started to feel a bit dizzy. A number of other conversations were taking place and snippets such as "The best thing about the good old days was that I wasn't good and I wasn't old" and "A little grey hair is a small price to pay for all this wisdom", could be heard. But as time went on the inmates and the staff were getting louder and louder as was the singing. The noise level was putting Derick off his driving and he said to Wayne, "can't you shut this lot up they're doing my head in?"

Wayne just sort of shrugged being a bit miffed at not being with one of the granddaughters, "I doubt they'd take much notice what with the booze and everything. I mean they've just been singing, 'if you're happy and you know it – it's your meds, if you're happy and you know it – it's your meds, and so on and on and on!"

Although Derick hadn't been drinking for some time, because of driving at night and also because of his own medication, Wayne had had no such qualms even though, technically he was on duty and responsible for getting everyone back safe and sound. He was staring into his drink and said in a rather sad voice, "even my relationship with whisky is on the rocks."

To which Derick replied, "good one that Wayne, Scotch on the rocks!"

Wayne just gave him a withering look and said, "why don't you just concentrate on your driving, if you can call it driving?"

Eventually the Manor Home could be seen in the distance. The hour long journey had took about four hours in all but because most of the inmates had managed to have a bit of a nap, on the coach, most were still fairly lively rather than being tired out. They started to stagger off the coach, singing at the top of their voices as the lights came on in the Home's windows.

They'd already had the whip round for the driver, which had been given to the cabbie, but as Wayne had 'got up peoples noses' there was no collection for him. Del stood up at the front of the coach and thanked them all for the thoughts even though he didn't have any money and there was a rousing round of applause. This was a reflection on people being grateful just to have made it back in one piece rather than any appreciation of Derick's driving.

Wayne was most put out and sulked in a corner of the coach as people disembarked not even bothering to say goodbye or 'see you next year'. He was thinking that they were a bunch of miserable old sods regardless of what he thought earlier on about their lively singing.

CHAPTER 19

The day after the day before

The next day was a Saturday and the inmates tended to sleep in later on the weekends than in the week for some reason. It seems that the routines embedded when they were at work were hard to break and so the weekends are treated as differently to weekdays even though generally the routines are pretty much the same.

This Saturday, however, seemed to take an awful lot longer to get everyone up and ready. One or two couldn't face breakfast having been up half the night on the toilet and such like.

Gertie, Mary and Elizabeth were amongst the worst because they were just not used to drinking, certainly not drinking such large amounts. They all looked deathly pale as they eventually entered the dining room. The general atmosphere was somewhat subdued and the other inmates who were already there seemed to be speaking in whispers which defeated the point as most of the inmates were hard of hearing. Even Cyril couldn't manage one of his jokes. When asked what they would like to eat they just groaned. Mary managed to ask for a cup of coffee and the other two just nodded to indicate that they would have the same.

The staff hadn't fared much better and both Mo and Priya were nursing headaches. Eric was nowhere to be seen and Brenda and Harry were feeling particularly rough because they had drunk a lot in a relatively short space of time, 'catching up with the others' was how they put it.

"Turn that music down can't you?" said Bert as he and the General made their tentative appearance in the dining room. The General just grunted his affirmation that the music should be done away with even though it wasn't particularly loud. The other inmates looked around and, as most of them couldn't hear any music, wondered what Bert was going on about.

Leeroy ended up helping Gertie into her seat and she was feeling very delicate indeed. Mary and Elizabeth didn't look any better but had managed to find their seats themselves.

"How did your grandson, Terry, and Elizabeth's granddaughter Becky get on last night?" asked Leeroy

"Oh, Becky's Cyril's granddaughter, I don't really recall her being there very much yesterday," replied Gertie with a faraway look in her eye.

"I meant Rebecca, didn't I?" said Leeroy.

Gertie sighed and said, "I don't know dear, it's all a bit confusing for me."

Leeroy decided to give up and went and got Gertie her breakfast which she took one look at and said, "I don't think I can face that this morning dear."

With the background, piped music turned down so low, that it was virtually non-existent, the increasingly noisy and aggressive clattering that was emanating from the direction of the kitchen could be heard more clearly together with the occasional cussing and swearing.

"What's all the noise about?" asked Soups Non-The-Wiser wincing.

Bert and the General both replied in unison, "it's Burnt Offering, he didn't have a single winner, or place, all afternoon yesterday," both looking around to make sure none of the management heard them even though it seemed to be common knowledge now that they and a few others had 'bunked off' to Redcar.

"Oh," said Soups, "I stayed with the main group in Whitby. I didn't know that there were going to be breakaway factions. Anyway I wanted to see how my forged museum tickets would fare. Turns out that they didn't need tickets for pensioners after all."

"Never mind old chap," said the General, "perhaps next year you can come to the races with us, perhaps cheer you up a bit."

"Might do," said Soups, "I used to be good at forging the tickets for the main race meetings, you know Ascot, Epsom and Cheltenham. The best tickets you know, for the best enclosures, no rubbish. Didn't cost a lot, just a bit for materials and that."

Bert and the General looked at him thinking about next year's outing to one of the major racing events instead of the seaside. "We'll have to discuss it with the management Old Boy," said the General looking decidedly interested in Soups for the first time.

Just then Eric came in with Peggy being the remainder of the racing contingent, Terry having gone home with Rebecca last night or rather earlier this morning. They were both very boisterous and although they had consumed as much alcohol as the others they still seemed to be 'bright eyed and bushy tailed'.

Harry and Eric had won quite a bit of money as had Peggy and the others all except Burnt Offering who was still making his views known judging by all the noise coming from the kitchen.

Eric said, "great day yesterday!" paused and then added, "what is that racket coming from the Kitchen?"

Harry replied that it sounded like Burnt Offering and that he was what would be termed a 'sore loser'.

The banging and battering of pots and pans continued as the inmates consumed what breakfast they could stomach and at a lot slower pace than usual. The stories relating to the Outing circulated with growing exaggerations on each telling. Elizabeth was saying, "has anyone seen Beryl this morning?"

Those within earshot just shook their heads and Elizabeth asked Nurse Brown if she had seen her.

Nurse Brown said, "I'm not surprised that she hasn't come down yet. The state she was in – the state you were all in! I've never seen anything like it. You should all be ashamed of yourselves."

"I think the Redcar lot were worse than us," managed Cyril.

"Never you mind about that lot. It's a disgrace, senior citizens behaving like unruly lager louts," said the Nurse.

"Don't you mean SAGA louts," said Young Joe, and everyone laughed.

"I know what I mean, thank you very much," replied Nurse Brown rather primly. "Why you couldn't all stay together I don't know. We had a lovely time on the beach. Very restful."

Elizabeth pipped up, "we didn't want restful – we get restful every day. No, we wanted adventure and the racegoers wanted excitement! Just because we're getting on a bit doesn't mean that we don't know how to live it up a little, you know?"

"That's all well and good, but with the amount of medication you lot are on, it's a wonder there wasn't a major catastrophe," the Nurse continued, "none of you should really be drinking alcohol at all, let alone the amounts consumed."

"Well a little of what you fancy eh Nurse?" said Cyril with a mischievous glint in his eye, "never really hurt anyone did it?"

Nurse Brown looked at the few who were listening and said, "It's not only drinking with the medication but the getting drunk as well. I mean it could be dangerous."

Mary said, "dangerous? I don't see how. A little drink now and again never hurt anyone. It's not as though we're drinking all of the time."

"No, a little drink probably not, you know the government guidelines are fourteen units of alcohol a week. And that's a limit – not a target. But those of you that went to the races (oh yes –

you needn't look like that - we know all about that) and the other lot that went to Robin Hood's Bay must have drunk about six weeks' worth in one go yesterday and last night!"

"Hmph, surely you exaggerate, Nurse," said the General.

"And don't think I don't know about your hip flask General! It's not only that, it's the state you were in when you got back! Young Joe decided he needed the toilet before going to bed……"

"What's so unusual about that?" said the General, "I mean most of us do."

Nurse Brown continued, "yes most of the inmates do go before bed but not in the wardrobe!"

There were a few smirks and the Nurse said, "also when Bert went up to his room and he decided he needed some fresh air as he was feeling the worse for wear from the all the drink he'd had. He opened a widow and promptly fell out! Fortunately though, although he's on the second floor, his window overlooks the community lounge roof and so he didn't have far to fall. Getting him back in to his room proved to be a bit of a challenge though I can tell you!" said the Nurse.

A number of the inmates turned to look at Bert who was trying to make himself invisible. A ripple of laughter broke out though and this broke the tension a bit until the Nurse continued, "that's not all! When we were trying to get you off the coach, those persons who were inebriated – and you know who you are- started messing about and as it had been raining it was slippery under foot and there were puddles. Well, Beryl slipped and went down into one of these puddles."

"Was she alright?" asked a concerned Mary.

"Oh she was fine. But she'd got it into her head though that she was drowning in the puddle and was trying to swim out of it," said Nurse Brown.

"There's more as well," she continued, "Peggy manged to get up to her room but then started screaming the place down. I would have thought that some of you may have heard her?" The Nurse looked around to a general shaking of heads and puzzled looks. "Well, I rushed into her and she was shouting, Tarantella, Tarantella, there's a huge Tarantella gone under my bed. Well I didn't know what to think. I didn't know what a Tarantella was."

"What was it, Nurse?" asked Bert shocked.

The Nurse waited for maximum effect and when she had everybody's undivided attention she said, "it was a spider! She'd meant to say Tarantula but mispronounced it!"

At this there was an uproar of raucous laughter followed by a lot of 'oohhs' and 'ahhhs' as the headaches started up again.

Breakfast continued with further stories about the previous days exploits. They were getting more and more exaggerated with each telling, to the point where some of the inmates wondered if they'd been on the same trip.

CHAPTER 20

An Inspector Calls

As the laughter died down and inmates took themselves off, mostly back to bed to sleep off the remainder of their hangovers, the front doorbell sounded and Eric went to open it. There stood two uniformed police, a PC and a WPC, together with a plain clothes man, who looked like he was CID.

Eric said, "hello, how can we help?"

The CID man held up his badge and said, "Detective Inspector Morgan of the North Yorkshire Police. Could I see the manager please?"

Eric replied, "which manager would that be then. We have a Catering Manager, a Store Manager, a Carers Manager, a......"

DI Morgan cut him off and said, "don't try and be funny with me sonny - who's' in charge here?"

"Well that depends," said Eric, "in charge of what?"

"Look are you deliberately trying to be obstructive, mate? Because I'm not very impressed and if you don't tell me who the main boss is pronto, you're going to be facing an obstruction charge – got it!"

The uniformed police were trying very hard not to laugh and Morgan knew that they were just waiting to take the piss when they got back to the station.

Morgan, who was almost old enough to be a resident at the Home himself, had been side lined a number of years ago now and the two young constables knew this. Morgan had made a number of disastrous decisions, mainly mistakenly releasing, known villains, who were to quote 'bang to rights' only to arrest them again later and repeat this process all over again.

He hadn't made a successful arrest for some time and the stress was beginning to show around his waistline and the thread veins in his nose. He was both tall and considerably overweight due mainly to the bottle of scotch that he tended to put away each evening. So he was in good company with most of the residents on that morning who were in a pretty similar state to him.

Although it was reasonably warm, Morgan wore a shiny suit, that had seen better days, and an overcoat which remained unbuttoned. He was also carrying a trilby hat which looked a bit battered and dated him considerably.

He sighed wearily and said very slowly, as though Eric was a retard, "the person in charge, I just want to see who is in charge of this.. this.. overall …Who's in charge?"

"Oh, why didn't you say so," said Eric brightly, "you'll want Ajay, "but I think he's tied up in a management meeting."

"Well bloody well untie him then," snarled DI Morgan and Eric went scurrying off as the two PCs snigged under their breaths.

Morgan looked at them and said, "do try and pay attention you two. I can't think why the 'Super' thought it necessary for all of us to come down here though for the life of me."

"I think the 'Super' was just trying to make sure we did things by the book sir," said the WPC with a smile.

DI Morgan just shook his head and mumbled to himself something about retirement not coming quickly enough.

Eric returned with Ajay who asked "what's all this about officers?"

"Do you have somewhere we can talk sir," enquired DI Morgan.

THE OUTING

"Yes, of course, come through to my office," replied Ajay and added, "would you like a tea or a coffee?"

"A cup of tea would be most welcome sir," replied DI Morgan with the two PCs nodding their agreement.

"Eric ask Leeroy or Sharon to get us some tea and bring it to my office please," said Ajay.

They settled in the seats around the main conference table in Ajay's office – the meeting room still held unpleasant memories of the visitors from the Local Authority and Social Services. Ajay said, "now then. How can I help?"

DI Morgan took a deep breath and said, "I understand that certain of your... your...clientele..."

"We sometimes call them inmates, Inspector, as a bit of a joke really, but we use the term inmates" jumped in Ajay.

"Very well, inmates then, were on a trip to Whitby yesterday, is that correct sir?" DI Morgan said as he glanced at his little black notebook.

"That's correct officer," said Ajay, "it was the annual outing and this year Whitby was chosen. Although I think we've been there before as well."

"I see sir, and can you tell me if a certain Kevin Collingswood went on this trip?"

"I'll need to get this list to check but I'm pretty sure Kevin would have gone. He doesn't socialise very much and we would have encouraged him to go on it. Why do you ask?" said Ajay.

"Well sir, we have reason to believe that your Kevin Collingswood had it away with... that is to say sir, he acquired certain goods without paying for them." DI Morgan said.

Ajay looked a little puzzled and said, "are you sure officer? I know Kevin can be a little eccentric and that he may forget to pay for his purchases but I can't believe he would deliberately set out to steal anything."

"Well the shopkeeper is adamant and has the CCTV to prove it." said DI Morgan with a smirk.

Ajay thought for a moment and said, "let's get Kevin in then and ask him! By the way what was it he is supposed to have taken?"

"Well that's just it sir, it doesn't make much sense really, he stole some pregnancy testing kits from a local chemist shop."

Ajay stopped and looked from one to the other of the PCs and the DI, "did you say....."

"Yes sir pregnancy kits, six of them in all," said DI Morgan.

"But what on earth would he want those for?" Ajay asked somewhat stunned.

"Let's have him in then and we might find out," replied Morgan looking a bit exasperated.

Kevin Collingswood was a small, mousey man of an indeterminate age. On closer inspection he would seem to be nearer to his seventies but it could be ten years either way. He was very slight so not only wasn't he very tall but also he only looked to weigh a few kilos. As the expression goes 'a strong gust of wind could have blown him over'. In spite of this he was quite nimble when he needed to be and looked very alert.

Kevin was wearing a shirt with the large, rounded collars that were fashionable about fifty years ago. The shirt actually looked that old as well because it needed a wash. On top of his shirt he wore what was known as a 'Val Doonican' cardigan (named after an Irish singer from the 1960s who used to wear such garments). There were a couple of holes in the cardigan and it had what looked like egg stains down the front. His ensemble was completed by a pair of 'bell bottom' trousers which were not only a size too big for him but had the widest bottoms almost making it look like he was wearing a skirt.

DI Morgan looked him over and shook his head thinking 'what

have we here? A very peculiar looking specimen and no mistake'. He'd done his research before setting out that morning into Kevin Collingswood or Kevin the Klepto as he was also known down at the station.

"Now then Kevin," he began, "what can you tell us about your visit to that chemist shop in Whitby yesterday?"

Kevin just looked at him with both his eyes and mouth wide open.

Just then Sharon arrived with the tea and chocolate biscuits. She must have been told it was the police because chocolate biscuits were only ever bought out for emergencies like important meetings with the police or government departments and such like. Not being too aware of the process of a police investigation, she jumped in and said, "you don't want to worry about Kevin, he don't mean anything by it," turning to Kevin she added, "do you Kevin?"

Kevin shook his head and was still looking a bit bewildered and Ajay said, "that's quite enough Sharon!"

"Come on Kevin, we just want to know what happened," Ajay continued.

The uniformed police started in on the tea and chocolate biscuits and DI Morgan thought he'd better get stuck in as well before they all went and so he picked up his tea with one hand and a chocolate biscuit with the other. Realising he couldn't also look at his notebook the Inspector tried to juggle all three things at once which meant the biscuit dropped into his tea, which then spilt onto his trousers and notebook, leaving him looking at a soggy notebook as he attempted to put his, now empty cup, onto the table.

Kevin and Sharon were both standing at the end of the table and together with the uniformed constables they were all trying to suppress the laughter starting to build up, aimed at the mess the inspector was getting himself in. The PC whispered something to the WPC about 'Inspector Clouseau' strikes again.

DI Morgan tried to muster up as much dignity as he could and refilled his cup. He was at a very delicate stage of 'dunking' a biscuit with the sodden bit precariously balanced as he attempted to bring it up to his mouth when Sharon blurted out, "we all know he takes things. He just can't help himself, can you Kevin? He's known as Kevin the Klepto because even he doesn't even know why he does it. It's not as though he ever pinches anything worth having is it Kevin?"

Kevin shook his head just as the dunked part of DI Morgan's biscuit broke off and landed in his lap. It was still hot from being in the tea and it added to the tea stain already there making it look like he wet his pants. He yelped and leapt up knocking over his second cup of tea. "Oh bugger," he said, then looked around and thought he better try and cover it up, "sorry about that it was just a bit of a surprise hearing that nick name. That's what he's known as down at the station as well."

Ajay said, "I'm sure we can sort this out." Turning to Kevin he asked, "do you still have the er..er... devices?"

Kevin stood there and just nodded.

"OK then, you and Sharon go and get them, and bring them back here," said Ajay.

The uniformed police were enjoying their tea and biscuits and seemed a bit oblivious to what was going on. They preferred to snigger and whisper about the Inspector already imagining how this would be retold to maximum effect back at the station.

DI Morgan was frowning thinking someone was going to do him out of his 'collar' as he termed an arrest. Trouble was these days there were all these do- gooders who thought a bit of therapy was the answer to everything. No, the Inspector, knew better – what was needed was a short sharp shock – that would sort them out!

Kevin and Sharon returned with the six pregnancy test kits still in their original wrapping and boxes. Kevin placed them carefully on the table as though they were the most precious possessions he had.

"There you go inspector, no harm done," said Sharon.

"It's not simply a case of returning them, young lady," said the Inspector, "Oh no. There are records to be completed and strictly speaking," he said, pointing at Kevin, "he should be arrested!"

"Surely there's no need for that. I think he may have just stopped his counselling sessions or not taken his medication." suggested Ajay. "Isn't there some way we could make reparation without it coming to an arrest?"

The uniforms stopped eating and drinking and watched DI Morgan carefully.

"Well," said DI Morgan, "I suppose we could let him off with another warning," emphasising the word 'another'. DI Morgan thought he must be going soft in his old age agreeing to counselling instead of getting him put in a cell.

"That would be most kind of you," said Ajay, "is there anything we can do? Here, inspector, please have another biscuit."

DI Morgan said, "I don't mind if I do," and took three and went on to say, "this is his last warning. I think the last time he had a final warning so this is his final, final warning. Anymore antics like this and he'll be going to prison."

"It's not prison he needs but some sort of psychiatric help!" Sharon shouted.

"That's enough Sharon," Ajay said, "please take Kevin back to his room and I shall speak to him later."

Kevin then left with Sharon not saying a single word throughout and as they were walking along the corridors Sharon whispered, "Kevin the Klepto strikes again," and laughed.

Kevin just smiled and walked onto his room wherein he got into bed and went straight to sleep dreaming of brightly coloured boxes there for the taking.

"Thank you for your understanding Inspector. I will make sure that this sort of thing doesn't happen again." Said Ajay. "It's a long way for you to come just for a few pounds worth of pregnancy kits. I mean it's not as if……"

"Actually sir," said DI Morgan as he referred to his notebook again, "there are one or two others matters that I need to take up with you."

"Oh, I see," said Ajay, "I didn't realise that there was something else as well?"

"Unfortunately sir that bit of shop lifting's not all I'm here about….I'm afraid there's a complaint, or perhaps I should say complaints, been made against other residents, inmates, here regarding their conduct in Whitby yesterday," said DI Morgan.

He went on, "There's the matter of being drunk and disorderly – and not paying for drinks. It seems that a number of your residents ran amok in Whitby yesterday evening. From the complaints we've received we've been able to ascertain that a good many of your group not only didn't pay for their drinks in the pubs that they visited but also were discovered stealing booze from a number of off-licences. I mean what is the world coming to when a pensioners outing turns into nothing short of a riot!"

"I can't believe it!" said Ajay, "are you sure you have the right outing. Our residents, I mean inmates, wouldn't do something like that."

DI Morgan said, "I have it on reliable authority, and I might add, backed up by CCTV cameras, that some of your inmates behaved like a bunch of football hooligans. Most of the people who have complained said that they couldn't believe that senior citizens would behave this way."

Ajay said, with his fingers crossed, "well we do have one or two , shall we say, more boisterous senior citizens and they're all encouraged to live life to the full here. But I wouldn't have thought they would break the law."

The uniforms were looking from DI Morgan to Ajay and back again, a bit like a tennis match. They still thought it all highly amusing but a welcome distraction from the usual police work that they faced on a day to day basis. This was much better than going up against someone with a knife or a gun which seemed to be the case more and more these days.

"As I've said we have eyewitness accounts and also CCTV footage. Unfortunately the descriptions that were given were, and I quote, 'old people, old men and old women, people who looked old', end quote. It's not really a lot to go on and the CCTV whilst it does indeed show old men and women it isn't clear enough to actually identify individuals," said DI Morgan looking at his notebook again.

"So what makes you think that it was our group doing all these things then?" asked Ajay.

"They were seen boarding the coach and the driver and tour guide, or whatever he was, were heard shouting that they had to get back here," replied DI Morgan. Also the granddaughter of one of the inmates, who happens to be in the force, was on the trip and whilst she wouldn't confirm or deny anything she did say that it 'got a bit lively at times!'

Ajay pondered this for a little while thinking good old Becky keeping her mouth shut and said, "I really don't know what to say. Look it's nearly lunch time and Burn....... Tony, our chef, normally does something special for Saturday lunch time and I was wondering if you would like to join us. All the residents will be together and perhaps you could have a word with them all before lunch in the dining room and let them know that this sort of behaviour will not be tolerated? The fact that individuals can't be identified needn't be revealed to them and perhaps a bit of a frightener that there may be further action would suffice as a warning?"

"Well that's very kind of you sir and it would be quite late us getting back to the station this afternoon and so, yes, lunch would be very welcome, thank you. I will take up your offer to address them all as well as to let them know that they have been let off with a caution." Said the Inspector.

"Of course, "Ajay went on, "we will make any compensation payments that are necessary to cover all of the costs these establishments have incurred due to this unruly behaviour and it goes without saying that we apologise unreservedly."

"Very good sir," said DI Morgan a bit awkward, "…….there's just one other thing though."

"What's that then Inspector?" asked Ajay thinking perhaps they'd got off too lightly.

"Well it's a bit embarrassing really," continued DI Morgan, "but two of your residents were seen 'flashing' and 'mooning' when your group were making their way back to the coach… and also I might add, when they were actually in the coach itself… 'flashing' and 'mooning' out of the windows sort of thing."

Ajay said, "I don't know what to say Inspector, we've never had that sort of behaviour here before."

Ajay looked around and hoped that no one could overhear what was being said as he knew full well that Little John and Big John flashing and mooning respectively was not a new thing. They were quite well known for it and Ajay could never understand how they had managed to get away with it for so long. He thought to himself the Inspectors got enough material here for a psychiatric convention!

"Let's go and have lunch and perhaps you can read them all the 'riot act' to stop this sort of thing ever happening again," said Ajay hopefully.

"Very good sir, I mean this sort of anti-social behaviour is more in keeping with criminal and hooligans rather than senior citizens isn't it? By all accounts they behaved like a bunch of juvenile delinquents yesterday!"

Ajay just nodded and then thought about it and started shaking his head as though it was all too unbelievable as he led the way through to the dining room.

After a delicious lunch of soup, beef wellington and treacle sponge DI Morgan and the uniforms were fit to burst and he said to Ajay, "you live very well here, having a lunch like this."

"Oh it's not every day that Burn….Tony cooks like this. Just that weekends are still regarded as being a bit special and so he does something nice of a Saturday and Sunday. Probably be a roast dinner tomorrow of some sort, with apple pie to follow." Ajay replied.

"Well it's very nice of you to invite us, thank you," said DI Morgan wondering how they managed to live so well without the proper government funding that he was continually reading about.

The two uniformed police officers mumbled their thanks as well as they got ready to leave. Other than the incident with the tea they didn't have a lot to relate back at the station but they could 'milk' that for all it was worth. This would lead to further stories about DI Morgan being retold amidst much hilarity.

DI Morgan went on, "I don't think you'll be hearing any more, particularly as you are willing to pay for what was taken and also to offer compensation for the inconvenience. So hopefully that should be an end to these matters."

"Well, goodbye Inspector," said Ajay.

"Goodbye sir, as I say I don't think you'll hear any more but I would remind your inmates that they have been lucky this time and that they need to behave themselves in future and hopefully they will be put off from doing anything like this next year after what I've said to them," said DI Morgan in a self-satisfied manner. "Just one more thing though - next year I wouldn't let them lose on Whitby again if I were you sir."

CHAPTER 21

A Reckoning

After the police had left, Ajay summoned, what he called, the finance team into his office in order to carry out a final reckoning of the costs of the Outing. It seemed almost inevitable that there would be more bills arriving from various establishments for all the booze pilfered and Ajay just hoped that there'd not be too many claims for compensation particularly from anyone witnessing the ordeal of seeing Little John and Big John's flashings and mooning's.

The finance team consisted of Ajay, Brenda, Henry, and Betty and usually held their meetings in Ajay's office once a month. However this was considered to be an emergency meeting and so, although it was a Saturday, Ajay thought the team should see what could be done in terms of damage limitation. He dreaded the press getting hold of some of these stories. The Home prospered because of its discretion and so any publicity was most unwelcome. This was most important especially in respect of some of the more borderline 'little earners' the inmates indulged in. Also following the recent visit from the Local Authority and Social Services the last thing he needed was a return visit from that lot to discuss the Outing.

Ajay explained to the others what had happened with the police earlier and that the Home was lucky to get away with warnings rather than face charges. He went onto say that they needed to be ready in case of any claims made against the Home or any of the inmates. He went on, "what we need is some of the reserves account to put some cash in ready to fend off any potential compensation claims. We'll need to pay for anything stolen as a matter of course and if we can offer compensation payments then that should sweeten it enough for it all to go away."

Henry said, "we need to make sure that any payments made are in 'full and final settlement', we don't want anyone coming after us later for any of the trauma suffered."

"I quite agree Henry," said Brenda, "we need to nip this in the bud, sort it out and move on. The last thing we want is for this sort of stigma to be attached to the Manor."

"So," Ajay said, "how are things looking Betty if we have to pay out some serious hush money?"

Betty had produced one of her famous spreadsheets showing all of the costs under different headings. It looked pretty impressive until the numbers were examined a bit more closely and then Betty's esoteric version of double entry bookkeeping took over which was completely indecipherable to most people.

"How come there's no costs for the coach, driver and tour guide?" asked Henry.

"Oh that's an easy one," said Betty relieved, "I paid for the coach, driver and tour guide last year, in advance, and so, as that's been and gone now, I didn't want to double count it. I think I've mentioned to you before the type of cash accounting that I operate"

"But you wouldn't be double counting it!" said Henry, "we need to include it so that we can see the full cost of the Outing." He went on, "what are all of these 'petty cash' entries against the names of the Matron, Nurse, Harry, Eric and so on?"

"Those are the floats, Henry," replied Betty.

"Floats, what floats? They don't have tills do they!" said Henry

"No dear, they're the floats for the incidentals, for the trip, silly. You know things they might need, refreshments, ice creams for the inmates, that type of thing you know?" said Betty beginning to get a bit flustered.

Henry shook his head in bewilderment.

Ajay, Henry and Brenda studied all of the amounts on the spreadsheet, which totalled to a considerable sum, and Brenda tended to pre-empt Ajay by talking over him but making the exact same points. It was curious to watch the pair of them as they both seemed to be thinking the same things at the same time it was just that Brenda could be a bit quicker off the mark in articulating their views.

So Ajay would start to say, "we need to... and then Brenda would jump in..." find out exactly what that money was spent on."

"Exactly!" said Ajay and Henry together.

Betty was becoming increasingly confused now. Why did they need to mess up her nice spreadsheet with all these other things that's what she wanted to know? It was all nice and neat and balanced and, alright, one or two amounts did look a bit excessive when looked at in black and white like that but as Betty always said, "you just need to see the bigger picture and then it will all make sense."

"Well," said Henry, "the coach, driver and that tour guide bloke were paid for last year, yes?"

Betty nodded

Henry continued, "and so were the lunches and the fish and chip suppers, yes?"

Betty nodded again

"So concluded Henry, "what exactly were these petty cash floats used for?"

"Oh that's easy to answer," said Betty somewhat relieved, "they use the floats for ice creams and refreshments as I've said."

"But they've had a hundred pounds each. How many ice creams are they expected to buy?" asked Henry a bit perturbed.

Betty considered this for a while and said rather sheepishly, "Oh it wouldn't only have been ice creams. They would perhaps buy a few drinks as well."

"Alcoholic drinks?" enquired Henry.

"Yes, if necessary," replied Betty

Ajay and Brenda both jumped in at the same time and said in unison, "if necessary?"

"Yes, if necessary," said Betty

"How can an alcoholic drink be necessary?" asked Henry.

"Well some of the inmates didn't like travelling in the coach and the only way to get them into it in the first place is the promise of a bit of booze if you see what I mean," Betty added rather sheepishly. "Anyway," she added, "you were there Brenda, you saw what the money was spent on."

Ajay, Betty and Henry all looked non-plussed as Brenda said, "well yes, I was there. Trying to stay out of the way most of the time as Matron and Nurse Brown seemed to have everything under control."

"Well clearly they didn't," jumped in Henry.

"What you need to realise is that there were outings within outings yesterday," Brenda went on, "there was a group that went to Redcar races and another that went to Robin Hood's Bay....."

"We didn't agree to any of this," jumped in Ajay.

"No, I know we didn't agree, mainly because we didn't know about it until it was too late," Brenda carried on, "both of these groups had members of staff with them that were buying the drinks and generally paying for anything they might need over and above the lunches and the fish and chips."

Ajay looked at Brenda and said, "well at least the majority of the party stayed in Whitby, so that couldn't have cost too much?"

Brenda shook her head and said, "the ones that stopped in

Whitby started off calmly enough on the beach, in deck chairs and having a paddle. But then some of them started to wander off. Kevin for example went walk about and, as you know, picked up a few things on the way. The two John's started to play up and Soups Baxter, I mean Tom, and Young Joe started asking for some more booze. So you can see the floats didn't last too long when you add up all of these activities going on."

Betty went on, "a number of the inmates don't travel very well and so the booze would sort of knock them out, particularly for the return journey, so they could sleep see?"

"How much was spent out of these 'floats'? I mean how much change did you get back?" asked Henry.

"Oh no, there's never any change back. I'm more likely to be given receipts for reimbursement of additional spending as all the float money was spent," said Betty chuckling to herself and mumbling, "change, no never any change, that's funny, change."

Ajay interrupted and said, "the police this morning informed me that several pubs and off licences were robbed of wine, beer and spirits by a group of old aged pensioners answering to the description of our lot! Why did they steal booze if there was enough money to pay for it all?"

Betty thought for a while and said, "some of our inmates can really knock it back you know and I suppose they may have got a bit confused about what was paid for. Perhaps there wasn't enough float to go around especially after they'd visited the shops as well. The Matron and Nurse probably wouldn't condone any more spending and so unless the other staff bought the booze out of their own pockets, for reimbursement later, of course, then the inmates probably didn't realise....." she tailed off.

"What shops are these, what's that got to do with it?" Henry asked in a concerned voice.

"I don't think we should look too closely at that side of things,"

Betty said, "the important thing is that all the money spent is recorded here, well nearly all of it, and what's more important it's come too far less than what was budgeted for."

Henry sighed, "it's only come in less than budget because you haven't included the coach and driver and tour guide and the meals."

"Oh yeah," said Betty almost to herself, "well, not to worry, all's well that ends well, as they say."

"But it's not all well!" shouted Henry.

Brenda said, "now Henry don't upset yourself, you know it's no good for your blood pressure."

Henry was shaking his head and Ajay said, "I think we'll have to leave it there. Thank you for all coming in and should we have any further claims then the surplus budget on Betty's spreadsheet will be able to pay for them." With Brenda almost echoing his words as he spoke them it sounded like the two of them were harmonising.

Henry was still shaking his head as he was lead from the room by Brenda as she tried to sooth him. He was overheard to say that he never witnessed "something which could turn out to have such a major impact on the Home." He went on, "even my subconscious realises this is all a perversion too far. What was supposed to be an old peoples outing tuned into a…into….a …. I can't even think of a word to describe it!"

Ajay turned to Betty and said, "how're the finances looking generally Betty from your point of view? We still got a healthy bank balance after taking into account these potential bills and compensation payments?"

Betty looked at the latest bank statements and said, "yes, and in a way, it's still a bit too healthy if you ask me. We need to hide a good proportion before the next audit. I can't understand these care homes that don't have enough money. A bit of creative flair and we have all the money we need."

"I know, but we are going to need a big chunk of it for the Outing," said Ajay, "Mind you, I have said to Head Office that some of them have no imagination…. and also… I suppose are a bit too honest for their own good. When the government have created such a mess then it's seems rude not to take advantage of it!"

"Quite right," said Betty, "we make claims on any one we can. It keeps it fair that way. The government, the local authority, social services, especially social services because they'd only waste the money otherwise. The grants, loans and other allowances all help and when we add in the token contributions from the residents, we are, to use a phrase, rolling in it!"

"Well they're all busy people in these organisations and so it's best not to bother them too much. That visit earlier in the week was a bit of a surprise though but I think we got away with it. It's best just to acquire the funds we need and leave these organisations in peace and also be discreet about it and we're good for some time to come all being well," concluded Ajay.

Betty said, "there is just one more thing though."

"What's that?" said Ajay.

"We shall need another outing to get rid of some more of the surpluses otherwise questions might start to be asked at some point which we could find difficult to answer," replied Betty.

Ajay sighed, "another outing? I'm not sure that I'm up to that just at the moment. We'll have to talk about it some other time. Perhaps next year?"

CHAPTER 22

An Inspector calls – again

DI Morgan and the same two uniforms appeared again a few days later.

Sharon opened the door to them and recognised the inspector and the two constables. She said, "Oh hello there, Inspector, have you come to see Ajay again."

"That's right, if you could just let him know that we are here please," said the inspector rather formally.

Ajay, "it's not about the Outing again is it inspector? I mean we've paid for everything taken now and have just agreed an awful lot of compensation to the Whitby people. I'd hate to think we've got to pay out anymore. It's come as a very expensive shock for our Home this Outing has."

"No Sir, it's not the outing this time, but I have received further reports about certain activities that seem to centre on your Home here," said the inspector a bit sheepishly.

Both the uniforms were watching him with a certain amount of barely disguised humour again. "They're just waiting for me to make a mistake," thought the inspector, "well I'll show them this time!"

Ajay was looking concerned and said, "certain activities, what certain activities are we talking about?"

"Well sir, where to begin, that's the thing. I have a list here," said the inspector referring to his notebook. "I happened to mention, to a few others at the station, that I had paid a visit and a number of other officers thought that I should return and address these issues that I have here." Quite what he meant was that he had been told off for not getting 'up to speed' with the latest developments concerning the Home which he should have done so before coming out to it the first time!

Ajay was thinking rapidly whether any of these 'activities' could be laid at his door as he waited for the inspector to continue. He was sure he could place any blame for misdeeds on others and could 'swerve' any accusations being directed at him. The SPV investment scheme was 'kosher', at least Henry had assured him it was. Nearly everyone at the home, staff and inmates alike had invested quite heavily in the scheme which was making handsome dividend payments based on the grants, donations and government loans the Home had received.

DI Morgan cleared his throat and then started to read at length from his notebook. He began rather dramatically, "the first matter relates to what some people would regard as insider dealing!"

"Really, what's that?" enquired Ajay, knowing full well what Elizabeth and her granddaughter Rebecca got up to. He'd even benefitted himself from some of this insider information by buying and selling the tipped shares.

"It's where people take advantage of information to buy or sell shares in companies before it becomes generally known," replied the inspector.

Ajay thought for a moment and said, "I can't see anyone here being able to do something like that."

"You'd be surprised, sir, at who gets up to this sort of thing. Now let me see, do you have an Elizabeth Shaw staying here?"

Ajay nodded.

The Inspector consulted his notebook once more and said, "and would I be right in thinking she has a granddaughter called Rebecca Shaw?"

Ajay nodded again.

"We have reason to believe that Elizabeth has been buying and selling shares on behalf of her granddaughter who just so happens to be a financial journalist."

Ajay just looked at the inspector with his mouth open and finally said, "Really? I think there must be some sort of mistake. Elizabeth is independently wealthy. She wouldn't need to indulge in any underhand or sordid ways of making money like that."

"I can assure you sir that there has been no mistake," said the inspector even though the two uniforms were looking a bit doubtful at this stage.

"Can I ask inspector, what evidence do you have that Elizabeth is mixed up in anything like this? Said Ajay.

"I'm afraid I can't reveal my source but we've had a tip off – well the Met. actually received the tip off," said the inspector.

"So who is it that has made this accusation?" asked Ajay.

"Well it was an anonymous tip off," the inspector replied

"You've come all this way on the basis of an anonymous tip off?" said Ajay rather incredulously. "I think we'd better talk to Elizabeth and see what she has to say for herself.

Elizabeth was summoned to Ajay's office and as she entered she was heard to say to Sharon "I had a really good hand which I've had to leave, you know? I could have cleared up there and it was a good pot."

Sharon said, "what were you playing? Was it bridge, I know a lot of the inmates like to play bridge."

"No it wasn't bridge, it was poker," said an exasperated Elizabeth, "the General had just raised and it looked like Bert and Old Joe were about to fold and so I was in with a very good chance of winning the pot."

"Oh," said Sharon, "I'm sure it won't take long. The Inspector is here again. You remember the one who came here before to talk about the Outing? Well he's come up on some further enquiries or something I overheard him say."

"Well it's no good now they'll all be onto another hand now," said Elizabeth as she entered the office.

Ajay introduced them and dived straight in saying, "the inspector here believes that you and your granddaughter are carrying out insider trading activities on the stock market. What have you got to say for yourself?"

Elizabeth summoned up all of the indignity she could raise and said very forcibly, "and what, may I ask, is your evidence for such outlandish accusations?"

The inspector looked at Ajay and then at this old lady, a well preserved old lady, but still old, although she seemed to be 'well bred' to use an expression.

He said, "we have received tip offs that you are buying and selling shares to coincide with your granddaughter's newspaper columns!"

"Tip off? Tip Off? What Tip Off is this then?" Elizabeth responded looking down at the inspector as though he was something she'd just scraped off her shoe.

"Just an anonymous tip off," said the inspector.

"I see," said Elizabeth, "so you don't have any actual evidence then do you?" Knowing full well that all of the transaction had been hidden through nominee accounts.

"Well no," replied the inspector somewhat taken aback, "but the tip off was from a very reliable source, I can assure you."

"I don't need any assurance Inspector," stated Elizabeth, "I completely refute his slanderous accusation and if you don't have any firm evidence then I suggest that you forget the matter or risk a slander prosecution being brought against you and your superiors for defamation of character. Myself and my granddaughter have nothing to do with this and unless you can prove otherwise, I bid you a good day! Good Day!" and with that she rounded out of the room so quickly that the Inspector was dumfounded and starred open-mouthed as Elizabeth left the office. The uniforms thought it was funny him being told off by an old lady and couldn't wait to tell the others back at the station.

"Well, erm…. that seems to have cleared that up but I also have to make enquires about the supply of some medications being delivered here," said the inspector desperately trying to regain some of his authority savaged by Elizabeth

"Oh yes?" said Ajay, "what's all that about then?"

"As far as I can make out," the inspector continued, "these are experimental drugs, in the prototype stage of development, that have gone missing. Most of them treat age related illnesses such as rheumatism, aches and pains, that sort of thing."

"I don't think any of our inmates would use those," said Ajay, "Matron deals with all of that side of things so let's have a word with her. Sharon could you see if Matron could pop in please?"

Matron came roaring into the office like a steam train and bellowed, "what's going on! Who's saying that I'm giving the inmates the wrong medication?"

The inspector was taken aback by the sheer force with which she'd entered the office and he took on the look of someone who's just received an electric shock. He managed to say, "we have reason to believe that some of the inmates here are receiving experimental drugs and that……"

"That's a load of nonsense," Matron butted in, "we have regular prescriptions. Everything is recorded and you are quite welcome to see the medical records!"

"These drugs," the inspector continued, "are what the pharmaceutical company calls prototypes. They are claiming that their patents are being breached, by forged agreements, enabling a supply to be released prior to being fully approved by NICE – the National Institute for Clinical Excellence – which of course should not be happening!"

Matron was fuming, "how dare you suggest that we administer untested drugs to our inmates. I'll have you drummed out of the force, making accusations like that!"

The uniforms thought this was good sport as they tried to hide their laughter as the inspector suffered a severe dressing down from Matron. She gave him 'both barrels' as it were starting with the Home's medical procurement practices and ending with the state of the NHS!

The inspector said, "well, can we just go and have a look at your storeroom then to make sure none of these items are there?"

Matron just shrugged and said, "I'll get Nurse Brown to show you. I'm having nothing to do with such a farce. Sharon could you ask Nurse Brown to accompany this inspector person to the medical store room please?"

In the storeroom the inspector and uniforms looked all through the different boxes and jars and tubes of ointment and such like all with their unpronounceable names. There seemed such a lot of it for a relatively small number of residents.

"Hello, Hello, Hello, what have we here then?" he said sounding every inch the copper he was and placing a wetted finger in some white powder to taste to determine what it was. "This doesn't look like the sort of medication you pick up over the counter from Boots the Chemist you know?" As he spread some of the white powder over the counter in the store room.

Nurse Brown looked at it and said, "no, I don't think you would get that from Boots."

The inspector smiled for the first time thinking, 'I've got em now, bang to rights, I've got em'. "well what is it then?" he said triumphantly.

"Its flea powder, for dogs," stated nurse Brown, "one of the residents used to have her dog with her when she first moved in but sadly the dog was a lot older than she was, in doggy year's equivalent, you understand?"

The uniforms and the inspector all stood there with their mouths open and nodding with the inspector thinking that he hoped that it wouldn't harm humans and trying to discreetly spit it out but unfortunately he'd swallowed the bit he'd tasted.

Nurse Brown continued, "yes the dog was very old and passed away shortly after she moved in here. We used to keep the dogs medication in here in that box that you've just broken open so's not to confuse it with human medication."

Back in Ajay's office a somewhat embarrassed and pale inspector skated over the medical supplies issue and was saying that he had received other comments about other supplies to the Manor – equipment and consumables – and food supplies were regarded as being suspect. "There's a little matter of some fish and meat going astray – I remember last time the meal I had here and I wanted to find out where your cook got his supplies," he said.

"Sharon ask Bur...... Tony to come into the office please," said Ajay.

Burnt Offering came thundering into the office a few minutes later, "what's they problem like man," he said with a slight Scottish lilt, that Ajay knew would get progressively worse as Burnt Offering could build himself up into a right old state. Ajay thought the inspector a very brave man, first taking on Matron and now Burnt Offering and said, "The Inspector here is asking about your kitchen supplies and particularly in respect of fish and meat. Is that right Inspector?"

"Wha's wrong wi me meat and fish. It can nae be off, I gets it straight from the market ye know?" replied Burnt Offering.

"Well we've had reports about stocks of meat and fish going missing from the local market here and, for that matter, other markets that supply the catering trade and in particular old people's homes," stated the Inspector.

"Are ye trying to imply that mah fish and meat has been nicked? Burnt Offering responded a bit louder than before.

The Inspector looked at Ajay and Ajay just shrugged as much to say, 'it's nothing to do with me', but nevertheless thought he'd better intervene before Burnt Offering reached critical mass and did something he might later regret. He said, "why don't you take the inspector into the kitchens and show him your store and the invoices that you have for your supplies?"

Burnt Offering screwed up his face no doubt suspecting some sort of Sassenach trick with this suggestion.

"Och aye," he said, "nae bother," and the Inspector followed him out.

Ajay said to Sharon, who had just been standing there after she had fetched Burnt Offering, "could you ask Brenda and Betty to come in please Sharon?" Sharon had stayed throughout the interviews because she hadn't been dismissed and thought it would be interesting to see what Matron and Burnt Offering had been up to. It was much more interesting that the cleaning she was in the middle of doing.

"Brenda, Betty, as you know we have DI Morgan back looking at one or two of our suppliers and he is currently with Bur…. Tony, in the kitchens looking at some of the food supplies. Now I need you both to have the same story as the rest of us. No slip-ups. We buy from whoever will give us the best deal and – this is particularly for you Betty – we always get invoices." Ajay was saying.

Betty gave a bit of a pensive look and said, "well we don't always have invoices Ajay sometimes it's a special, one off, deal that in-

THE OUTING

volves cash and no questions asked."

Ajay shook his head and said, "if the Inspector wants to see invoices he shall see invoices. Brenda go and see Burnt .... Tony.... Oh to hell with it... Burnt Offering and find out who his main suppliers are and how much he's spent with them recently. Pass the details onto Betty and Betty you can 'mock-up' a couple of invoices can't you?"

"Well, I've done it before Ajay," said Betty all innocently.

Ajay pretended that he hadn't heard that remark and just said, "come on chop, chop, let's get moving."

Meanwhile Burnt Offering had discreetly informed Brenda of the names of his main suppliers whilst the Inspector examined the storeroom. After Brenda left Burnt Offering went over to see what the Inspector was up to.

The Inspector said, "this is all of your stock is it? There's no sub stores anywhere?"

Burnt Offering was beginning to simmer a little at the Inspector who seemed to be being deliberately obtuse even when Burnt Offering was able to reasonably articulate his ordering and buying policy.

"OK," the Inspector said, "for now anyway. I'll go and see Ajay to see if he can throw any more light on the situation."

Burnt Offering just growled and continued to simmer away as he prepared lunch mumbling incoherently under his breath.

"Ah there you are Inspector," said Ajay, "we're just off to lunch," indicating Brenda and himself, "I wondered if you and your colleagues would like to join us. By the way where are your colleagues?

"Yes I would like to join you for lunch, but the Uniforms won't be able to. I've sent them on a little errand," said the Inspector with a bit of a gleam in his eye.

Ajay wasn't sure if this was to do with the Home or sweet revenge on the Uniforms who had been playing the inspector up again ever since he arrived.

Over lunch they discussed the situation generally regarding supplies and specifically in respect of the food the kitchen ordered.

Ajay said, "I can assure you that's it's all above board and accounted for. You could have a word with Betty after lunch and I'm sure she will have the necessary paperwork to confirm that everything is in order. Isn't that right Brenda?"

Brenda nodded as she ate her lunch and said, "yes I'll take you to her after we've finished and I'm sure she can clear up any queries you may have."

After lunch Betty took him through her unique bookkeeping system which gave him both a headache and eye strain. As she explained the paperwork and processes she followed, his headache turned into a migraine and during the showing of a mountain of largely, falsified invoices he felt himself going comatose.

"I think we'll leave it there Betty," said the Inspector feeling the need to lie down in a darkened room.

Just then Ajay appeared and said, "are you alright – you look a bit pale?

The uniforms arrived back, from Whitby, it appeared the inspector wanted to make sure that all of the landlords and shop keepers were happy with the reimbursements and compensation payments that had been made.

The uniforms were unhappy because they'd missed out on lunch and so were asking what the inspector had come up with (not a lot he'd replied), when Ajay said, "did you say earlier that you also wanted to have a chat with Leeroy about the investment scheme we run here? It was the Home's accountant Henry of course that hit upon the idea but Leeroy is the one who deals with all the administration and makes sure that the correct monies go to the correct places.

"Yes of course," said the inspector desperate to try and find something he could report back on. Leeroy was wheeled into the office pretty quickly by Brenda.

Leeroy had helped to administer the SPV bonds scheme investment and dividend payments ever since Ajay and Henry had set it up. It was a 'nice little earner' for him. Leeroy said, "it's all documented Inspector and every penny, in or out, is recorded by Betty. Have you met Betty Inspector?"

The Inspector moaned and thought, "not again", he said, "I'm sure that will be OK Leeroy. I've already had a long session with Betty and I think I've got the hang of what she was saying. So that's fine, thank you," he said, giving up, and with that Leeroy was dismissed.

"I'm so glad everything has worked out OK," said Ajay, "and it's nice to see you again Inspector. Do feel free to call in at any time."

"I think I've probably seen enough but there is one last thing that I ought to mention," said the Inspector.

"Oh and what's that?" asked Ajay thinking that they'd got away with everything.

The Inspector consulted his notebook once more and said, "It's a bit unusual to come across this sort of thing but a number of forged documents have turned up."

Ajay frowned but said nothing, thinking this is Soups non-the-wiser, I'll bet.

"Yes we've had a number of documents and some event tickets referred to us by different people which have turned out to be forgeries. They're very good forgeries but forgeries nevertheless!"

Ajay said, "what makes you think this is anything to do with us?"

The Inspector replied, "well there was an envelope with this address on it that had a forged document in it."

"what sort of forged document was that?" asked Ajay.

"It was actually a bearer bond," said the Inspector, "most unusual. A very elaborate forgery because the bond certificate was quite old with intricate lines and swirls and all sorts of squiggles. A very complicated design to try and copy really."

"Squiggles?" enquired Ajay, "what sort of squiggles?"

"Well, like wavy sort of lines," the inspector indicated by waving his arms about.

Ajay thought that Soups had out done himself this time trying to be too clever by half, he always liked the challenge of that sort of document. He said "No I don't think that would be anything to do with us Inspector, I mean anyone could have picked up an envelope that could have been in the rubbish and reused it."

"Hmm….that's what I thought…but you know, the powers that be and all that…," suggested the inspector much to the delight of the uniforms who were standing behind him.

The uniforms were thinking that the Inspector resembled the Peter Sellers character of Inspector Clouseau even more now, with not even a single arrest to show from all of the leads and tip offs he had been following up on. They thought it was incompetence bordering on a level of idiocy difficult to understand. The only saving grace for this visit was that he hadn't wet his trousers this time. They both concluded that senility is going to be a fairly smooth transition for him.

Both the uniforms were looking at each other wondering how the Inspector was going to bounce back from this. He'd basically accepted all of the explanations at face value without really putting too much pressure on. They could see the writing on the wall and thought he just can't keep failing to get arrests – he's nearing retirement now and he'll be forced out soon.

With that and Ajay's 'well-wishes' the Inspector and Uniforms bade goodbye to Ajay, Brenda and Betty who had come to see them off. Ajay mopped his brow when they were gone and said, "thank goodness they've gone. I don't think I could go through that again. They're getting too close to for comfort and so I think we need to tell the inmates that they need to be a bit more careful with their extracurricular activities in future!"

CHAPTER 23

The Inspector calls - yet again

It was some time later that year as all memories of the Outing were a bit distant and thoughts were turning more towards the Christmas festivities that the Home indulged in each year. As Christmas wasn't far away now the inmates were beginning to get excited as Christmas at the Manor was always a lavish occasion with no expense sparred.

"Look at them," said Matron, "they get more like children every day."

"Oh they are just full of fun. It's nice to see old people still enjoying themselves and getting excited about things," replied Nurse Brown.

Ajay, Brenda, Henry and Betty had carried out an end of year review and the SPVs were working very well, the funds kept on coming and the end of year surplus was still looking very healthy even after paying for next year's outing.

Ajay was saying that, "other homes, associated with CHC, have expressed a wish to get involved with us, here at the Manor, to see how we go about getting grants and contributions from the various agencies. Although I not sure we want to share our unique way of………"

Just then the door bell sounded and they could see that it was DI Morgan standing there – again!

"Hello Inspector. What's this third time lucky? Where's your uniform escort?" Said Ajay as he added, "have you come to enquire about the Outing or those supplies we were talking about before Inspector," asked Ajay innocently.

"Well neither actually, I've come to see if you have room in your home for an ex Detective Inspector?"

Ajay was taken aback and said, "are you sure it's the sort of place where someone of your… your…. er…..sensibilities will fit in?"

"Oh, I know what you mean Ajay, but I'm not a copper now you know. You might have thought that you pulled the wool over my eyes. What with the Outing and, shall we say, certain goings-on. The uniforms laid it on think back at the station and I was asked to retire. I'd thought that, with all that's happening in the world today, a few indiscretions, shall we say, could be overlooked, don't you?" said the ex-Inspector.

"I couldn't agree more DI Morgan and I'm really pleased that you see it that way and of course I'm sure we could find accommodation for you here. If that's what you want. Isn't there a Mrs Morgan?" asked Ajay.

"No I'm on my own now the wife left me some time ago. Too busy pursuing a career in the police and so the job put paid to my marriage as it does to so many others these days. So I'm on my own and I know you have a number of rascals and rogues here, and that's just the women, but I think I could fit in," said the ex-inspector. He went on, "I don't think I've ever seen such a bunch of OAPs that are so full of life in spite of some of their advanced ages. I know they sail close to the wind with their various activities but the most important thing is that they haven't given up. You know I've been into other old people's homes and they are literally 'God's waiting rooms' with people sitting round just staring into space. Its soul destroying! At least here they seem full of life and fun even those who aren't always the full shilling so to speak. Yes, I know, legally they can be, and have been a bit shall we say 'naughty' but I'd rather be somewhere where's there a bit of life going on rather than just sitting around doing nothing."

"Oh we definitely have a lively 'bunch' as you put it," said Ajay, "because of some of these er.. extra activities, shall we say, we are able to run this home on a private enterprise basis. Which means we are fortunate enough to generally have plenty of funds for what we need to do. The inmates make contributions and we have charitable donations and certain monies from government agencies and the like and Betty our book-keeper, you remember Betty don't you? Well she's very good at keeping tabs on the monies due to us and so on. Coupled with the supply contracts that we have been able to secure with some of the relatives of the inmates, we are, to coin a phrase, 'sitting pretty'."

"Well as far as I'm concerned providing there's no physical violence then there's no harm done. I did have a discrete chat with Cyril the last time I was here and he assured me that I'd fit in. The way you and Betty run the Home and the help the inmates with their provisions is of no concern to me – not anymore. Let me know what sort of contribution you will need from me and I will happily 'chip in' for my board and keep. You can assure the residents that they can be at ease in my company as I shall not be paying any attention to what they get up to," said the ex-inspector, "and I shall certainly not be going back to the station ever again!"

"That's very reassuring ins….., you know I can't keep calling you inspector or ex-inspector or even DI Morgan, what is your first name?" asked Ajay.

"Oh, it's David, Dave actually," said the ex-inspector beginning to feel at home already.

"OK, Dave, let's get Brenda, my assistant, to show you round and then we'll complete the paperwork and you can move in later today," said Ajay leading him to where Brenda was, he added, "the full works Brenda, show him the full works."

CHAPTER 24

All's well that ends well

Dave Morgan settled in very nicely and his stories about his life in the police were listened to very attentively by the inmates of the Manor. This was mainly so that they wouldn't get caught out in the same way as those that had had their collars felt by Dave in the past. He and Cyril were like a double act telling stories and cracking jokes.

Initially there was a slight mistrust. He had been a fully paid-up member of plod after all and "you need to remember that he's been in the force for a long time and it's going to take him time to adjust" as Cyril was wont to say.

After the initial awkwardness Dave was accepted into the fold and he even became interested in one or two of the dubious activities. He especially liked helping Elizabeth and her granddaughter Rebecca. He reasoned that a bit of insider trading never really hurt anybody and what little money he made out of the deals could well be afforded by the city types that he used to interview over some other misdemeanours from time to time. He remembered the times when these types used to buy a brand new Porsche with their annual bonuses and then promptly smash it up because of all the cocaine that they had snorted!

Some of the women inmates initially referred to him as "that nice inspector person who came to give us a talk about the teddy boy hooligans who ran amok in Whitby that once." He hadn't really got the heart to tell them that it was actually them who'd been behaving like hooligans during the Outing.

Dave Morgan stayed clear of the buying and selling of the supplies for the Home reasoning that the instigators of this little free market endeavour were living on borrowed time and that sooner or later the balloon would be going up in that particular area. He reasoned that he needed to distance himself from such activities being a bit too 'free enterprise' for his liking.

He liked the horse racing and so got on famously with the General who thought the police were just another part of the army – they wore a uniform after all. He also got on with Bert and Gertie and Harry all of whom were regular punters on the races. They'd started the plotting for the next outing and many discussions were held on which race course they should go to.

With Christmas approaching fast, thoughts of next year's outing started to be voiced and Dave was looking forward immensely to next year's trip. After all the aggravation of this year's escapades he felt sure that he would have a good time and just hoped that the inmates would be a little bit better behaved.

Various suggestions were being put forward of where to go from the exotic (Scotland or Wales) to the more down to Earth (Blackpool). Most of the inmates were in favour of some coastal area provided there was a racecourse nearby and 'places of interest' to explore.

Ajay said to Betty, "You'd better reserve Wayne and Derick again. It looks like it's going to be Whitby again the way it's going because no one can make up their mind. It'll have been long enough for the people and shopkeepers in Whitby to have forgotten about this year's escapades, hopefully, and so I think we'll get away with it."

Brenda was virtually repeating what Ajay had said word for word and they both finished speaking at roughly the same time. Betty just smiled and said she would get onto it. She had already paid in full for the coach and tour guide again. She would just get onto the places in Whitby and was sure that by offering suitable financial inducements the good people of Whitby would invite them back again. The only thing would be the floats to sort out a bit nearer the time.

There had been some discussion on this before and, at one of the meetings, Henry enquired, "and where is it that the outing will be next year then?"

"Why, it'll be Whitby," they all said with a laugh together.

So the Manor continued with Betty's unique bookkeeping skills and the resident's extracurricular activities. There was no shortage of money and the residents lived life to the full thanking their lucky stars that they were where they were.

Ajay remarked, "it's not only the money you know? It does help but the zest for life that all the inmates possess, even those who were suffering from chronic illness, enables them to enjoy life to the full.

As one inmate who paraphrased the quotation by Dylan Thomas, said, "do not go gently into that good night....... but go kicking and screaming!"

Brenda concluded by saying, "I think, myself, that it's summed up in Hamlet quite well and quoted, - 'there is nothing either good or bad, but thinking makes it so' - don't you think?"

THE END

Printed in Great Britain
by Amazon

66274482R00108